"I apologize for the intrusion. I'll come back later." Lana pivoted at the door, but Vivian stalled her.

"No need—you're right on time to be introduced to our client. This is the account I told you about last night, Lana. Garrett Wilcox, Lana Stone."

All delicious six foot of him stood to take her unsteady hand, but she danced out of his reach, around the chair. Trying to cover mortification at the idea of working anywhere near this man, she attempted to be polite.

"Mr. Wilcox. I'm sure you will find Reed Agency a valuable asset. We have a lot of talent housed under our roof."

He recovered his unanswered handshake easily, but he gave her a look. His lips curving into a sexy smile that hinted at secrets.

"I admit to being captivated by your talents, Miss Stone. Vivian was sharing some of your more celebrated ad campaigns, and I've seen some of your work in magazines I enjoy." He dipped his head at her. "I appreciate the hospitality synonymous with your company. It shines through. You're quite talented."

Was he taunting her—daring her to comment on their kiss? Hah, not a chance!

Dear Reader,

Warmest greetings! I appreciate you for checking in here at Riverbend Falls amid the festivities of the season. I've been breathing life into this town for years, and I am so excited to be able to share it with you. I hope you find the adventures to be as genuine and fun as I do.

What I love most about Lana is the way she makes decisions based on her needs despite pressures to just "do something."

I love how Garrett consistently chooses happiness. There is a bright light shining every day if we look for it. Lana and Garrett face real life decisions and together, remind me there is a marvelous gift in the many ways we share love with each other.

I'd love to hear from you! Check-in at www.delilahsdiction.com and sign up for my newsletter! While you're there, follow me on Pinterest to see the photos I use to inspire me, or at my Facebook page, where I enjoy "Sharing My Journey" with each of you!

Delilah

Lana's Leap

Riverbend Falls ~ Book 1

Delilah Dewey

ISBN: 979-8-9873319-0-3 (Paperback)

LANA'S LEAP

Copyright © 2022 Delilah Dewey

All rights reserved. This book or any portion thereof may not be reproduced or used in any manner whatsoever without the express written permission of the publisher except for the use of brief quotations in a book review.

This is a work of fiction. Names, characters, businesses, places, events, locales, and incidents are either the products of the author's imagination or used in a fictitious manner. Any resemblance to actual persons, living or dead, or actual events is purely coincidental.

Printed on Demand in the United States of America.

First printing, 2022.

Delilah's Diction
delilahsdiction@gmail.com

www.delilahsdiction.com

Dedication

To those of You who have believed in me all along,
I know You. I love You.
Thank You!

This has been a long journey, and my writer's heart has been touched by so many… I am grateful to the friends I've made in the many seasons of my life who shouted a word of encouragement or sent endless waves of you can do it! Thanks for being you!

To the writers and readers in my circles who have shared their successes and failures in writing and in life over the years, thank you for being an inspiration.

I especially want to thank my family for putting up with all the personality quirks of having a writer in the family, you know how I am! I love each and every one of you from the bottom of my heart. Thanks for letting me be me!

Chapter 1

"I'm glad my timeline isn't a deal breaker. I'd planned to wait until after the holidays to get started, but I'd like to be up and running by March, and booked solid by Memorial Day. Things have already started rolling for me." He paused, thinking this was for all the marbles. "You think this is doable for your staff?"

"I'm certain," Vivian Reed said, her hand on his arm as she leaned into him. "If it presents a problem for my best agent, darling, I'll work for you myself."

Garrett Wilcox chuckled, charmed. She was likely his grandmother's age—and well preserved at that. For a small town, her ad agency had a big reputation, and he hoped to recruit a little help to navigate the community, as well as a right-hand man for a few months while he focused on bringing the dream to life.

He'd arrived in Riverbend Falls, Missouri a few days ago, but he'd been waiting years. His grandparents announced plans to retire and travel just this last fall, and he knew this was it. He purchased the riverside campground they'd owned for 40 years, and everything on it. The land deal with Stone was cooking. His dream of building a classy rustic vacation resort was for real happening. To be done with the long-distance dreaming—top shelf.

Vivian was wily about specifics, though. She agreed to lend

him a "well-equipped tool," insisting without a trace of vanity that her agent was the best. If the agent was half as good at selling his dream as this gal was at selling her agents, he was going to get what he needed. Dream big, act fast. Worked for him.

"And if your agent would consent…"

"Garrett, honey," Vivian drawled, a crafty gleam in her eye, "for now, nobody's consenting to anything, except a bit of dancing and Christmas cheer. No need to fret. For folks who've lived in the Ozarks as long as Wilcox's, we'll see your needs met. We can handle business in my office tomorrow morning, say eight?" Vivian smiled in anticipation of his nodded agreement. "Good. Are you sure you don't want to dance?"

"It's a fine offer, Ms. Reed, but if I monopolize much more of your time, those fine fellows over there won't get to set your feet on the dance floor." He waved at a group of old timers watching the two of them curiously.

"You'll certainly make a charming addition to our little town, darling. I'm delighted you chose Riverbend Falls for your project. Now you let me know if you need any help settling in." She batted long eyelashes, and Garrett hid his grin. "Send hellos to Jasper and Emily for me, and thank the old codger for the glowing recommendation."

"I certainly will. I'll be by at eight tomorrow. It sure was a pleasure meeting you, ma'am." With a good feeling, Garrett stepped away, angling toward the exit.

He was buzzing with energy despite a general weariness from the excitement. They had set several cabins that morning, and it was a good start. As he cruised through the room, he noticed people quieting down as he walked by. There probably weren't many strangers here. He must seem rude. Garrett detoured to the quaint little "bar" set up near the bandstand to do some socializing. He would get to know a few of the locals before rousing the quiet town.

With a wish for a cold beer or perhaps a good whiskey, he eyeballed his selections and chose soda over punch. He spied some unopened champagne in the corner, but he wasn't going to ask the seasoned woman serving the punch to open it.

He tried to make small talk with two older fellows in flannel shirts standing against the wall, but after a few attempts at pleasantries only gained him a few wary nods, Garrett simply stood by them, hoping to look friendly.

With a deep breath, he took a swallow of his drink, and for the first time, noted the scene. The decorations made him think of the traditional Christmases he'd craved growing up. It wasn't the way his parents did things, though. Winter had iced over the room, which was hard to manage with the warm wild wind blowing up leaf tornados outside despite it being December. Crazy weather in this river town...

A flash of glitter and flesh had his next swallow catching in his throat. Garrett noticed an athletic blond wearing a pale slip of a dress and knew it was the girl with the sunny halo that had toyed with his dreams. She burst from the shadows like a sunbeam reflecting through an icicle. Her dress revealed a luscious amount of toned back, and Garrett restrained a ripple of desire to touch. She seemed oblivious to the hungry eyes she was inspiring in most of the men in the room as she headed toward the area he'd just vacated.

He wet his lips with another slow swallow as he watched her slim hips sway to the beat of the music. She was the girl. One year, when he was twelve, he was allowed to summer here with his grandparents. He spent much of his time at the riverbank, playing, and had seen her through the brush as she sang and danced to a music all her own. It was another year or two before he really noticed girls, but her memory had stayed with him. Maybe he hoped she'd still be here when he came back. She was—and she was all grown up.

He watched the warmth she spread to those around her. It radiated from glass green eyes, throwing out green gold sparks of light every time a smile lit her face. She stopped often to hug or chat with someone. She was smoking hot.

He could barely keep his eyes off her, though he knew better. Picking up chicks in a small town was a bad move. He knew enough to know that. What he needed was a sense of the town before he started fitting it to his needs. It was conservative. A couple of churches and a bank. Little Mom and Pop shops. Antiques and what-nots. A town that rolled up the sidewalks about dark-thirty. His Pap was already muttering about him applying for a liquor license. Things might get complicated. What he needed right now was to keep his head clear...

He couldn't help himself—caught in the net she'd cast over him yet again. They'd never shared a word that long ago summer. In fact, she'd not known Garrett had watched over her, wondered about her, delighted by the creative way she played... He was certainly not going to admit it. If he just introduced himself, he'd see he'd built her up in his mind. That she was an ordinary pretty girl. He could handle that. Couldn't he? He should walk away.

She stopped to talk with Vivian, and a few strands of honeyed blond hair fell from a fancy braid as she laughed, framing her face. He wanted closer to her, appreciating all the angles gifted by the little dress. Garrett did not turn away, but he was reluctant to move forward. He should just treasure the sweet memory. Resting his drink on a small table, he walked toward her and stopped again. A woman would distract him from his project, and he had a lot of ways he could mess this up and end up with a million-dollar investment and no revenue.

Maybe he didn't want his childhood fantasy to collapse. He stood in the middle of winter, staring at the sun. And he was being ridiculous. What could be the harm in introducing himself? He needed to fit in, right? When Vivian left to dance with an older fella, leaving the golden girl alone, Garrett quit wondering and decided to find out.

Lana was admiring the results of her feverish work over the past two weeks. This was her third year setting up for the town's annual Christmas party solo, and she was getting good at it, she'd decided. A little hollow nestled in her heart, despite the splendid success. It never really went away, but she sensed it more keenly this time of year.

A heat hit the bareness of her back and she was surprised

someone had so fully invaded her space bubble. She turned to the man standing directly behind her. Something elemental shifted. Everyone's merrymaking faded to a dull hum. Her peripheral vision got kinda hazy, and she barely noticed.

Vaguely, she thought this must be her boss's date, since he and Vivian had been talking when she first noticed him. He was the only Greek God in the room wearing Armani. Her brain betrayed her. She lost herself in eyes a deep shade of steel blue. They promised a sensuality that normally sent her fleeing in another direction.

She shared every breath with him, dragging through time. He wore his raven-black hair shaggy, seemingly in danger of hiding his eyes, and it disrupted his polish with an impish impression. Lana had an urge to run her fingers through his hair. It looked soft, contrasting his lofty frame, which looked so very hard. She knew she needed to break the spell. Now would be good.

"Hello. Have we met?" There was something familiar about him, but she knew they'd never met because her heart had never hammered in her chest like this before.

"Dance with me." His rough voice caressed her like sand on naked toes as he caught her hand. Her legs were liquid, carrying her into his arms. He drew her closer, overpowering her senses. Everything happened fast; Lana had no time to respond to her howling subconscious. Intense heat filled the air between them, though there was little actual distance between their bodies.

She was a competent, strong woman. Except her strength was gone, and she was nothing but the woman. Right now, she was alluring, even... sexy. Lana's brain kept trying to breach the haze—danger, danger, Will Robinson—but the dream had her. She didn't want to let go of the flood of rare emotion.

He smelled like expensive cologne, and Lana's senses spun dizzily as the hard body beneath his jacket pressed close to her cheek. His long fingers rested on her bare back, and they seared her skin with a flame her body begged to be dipped in. Delicious, but sooooo dangerous.

Lana realized she was nestled into his muscular arms. She

lifted her face from his chest and noted another song starting. She needed to ground herself, find a little reality check. She stepped away, but he pulled her close again. His warm breath teased the flesh on her earlobe, then he whispered in her ear.

"Stay a little longer."

The command should have spiked her ire, but he drew her to him like flame draws attention in the dark. She let pleasure override her common sense and just nodded against him, promising herself she'd listen for the next break in music. His fingers were lightly kneading the skin at her waist, and Lana was floating. It was like a dream, but better than her usual dreams. She felt an embarrassed blush creeping up her neck as she realized her body was subtly wrapping around him. She inched back, but it didn't last.

"Just one more dance," she mumbled to herself, leaning into him a little more. Lana swayed, mesmerized, thinking she shouldn't be so agreeable. She didn't know him at all, yet they were… connected. The air between them was so hot he was nearly a second skin, as if they were one and he knew she needed more of him. Nuzzling the skin just below her ear, he touched his lips to her neck, a feather-light kiss so exquisite she thought she might explode. Then she did.

She pushed at him, muttered, "What is your deal?" Her decibel level picked up, and she knew panic was setting in. "What do you think you're doing? Geez… can't even dance without losing yourself," she snapped, then stilled.

She took a deep breath, closed her eyes, then opened her eyes and pinned him with her most haughty glare. She knew, she'd practiced. Garrett was staring into her eyes with intent, clearly fascinated by her level of crazy.

"Kind sir, the music has stopped, and I think a… gentleman like yourself might do well to find his date." She spun, but he caught her hand.

She turned back to demand he let her go and ran into his delicious looking mouth. Literally. The way he was standing, when she turned, she kissed him. And he did not let the opportunity pass to give her a tantalizing taste of him. Then he calmly stepped back and caught her other hand, leading her stiff body into a gentle sway. Her traitorous body actually went along with this plan, and she swayed just once before she backed away. There was no haughtiness now. She was just desperate to get away. This was what mortification tasted like! And what his mouth tasted like...

"Don't run away. Tell me your name?"

"Hah!" she said, her cheeks hot. "You will have nothing more from me, sir!" Dropping a curtsy, she backed up out of his reach. What was that? "I've got to go," she said and hurried away so fast she was nearly running. Would run if she hadn't worn the absurdly tall heels.

That man was unbelievable! And she'd curtsied like he was a king instead of some stray Vivian dragged in. He'd gotten all the way under her skin. It was humiliating. She'd kissed a complete stranger in front of everybody. Tongues would wag...

Unfortunately, halfway across the room, that was started by Cynthia, the town's gorgeous busybody.

"Fabulous decorations, Lana. You always do manual labor so well." Her saccharine voice grated on Lana's nerves. "That's some dress—you look straight out of Brides magazine. You should have come by my shop... I could have helped you pick something more you." She pretended to scan the room, then her nails. "What happened sweetie, your hot date run out on you?"

An unexpected ally saved her, interrupting. "I thought I might find you here. Let's grab a table." Tad Stone pointedly ignored the woman who had been a childhood crush. "It's good to see you, sis."

"Wow, you're here. What a great surprise!"

"Dang, you're a sight for sore eyes, kiddo."

"It's the dress," Lana said, modestly smoothing the sumptuous ivory silk. Last quarter's bonus had incentivized the splurge. It had been pricey, but the freeing feeling inspired by the elegant curve-hugging dress seemed worth it. After her dance floor fiasco and Cynthia's catty comments, she was thinking so a lot less.

"I have something I need to talk to you about."

They settled at a small table in the corner. "Do you want some punch?" she asked.

"Champagne? We can celebrate my being home."

Lana shifted her attention back to her brother. "I don't know… Vivian's got a client interview in the works for early tomorrow. I'll need to prepare."

"One glass. I just saw them opening a case, and with this group of teetotalers, someone will have to drink it." He grinned, jumped up, and came back with two plastic champagne flutes and grandly handed her one, raising his for a toast. "To being home for the holidays."

"Yeah, home." Despite being determined not to indulge in self-pity this season, she thought of her apartment, where His Lady of Destiny awaited. It was a Viking romance and she would just sink into it. She would be fine.

"So what's this about?" Lana dreaded her brother's intentions. "How come you didn't tell me you were coming for Christmas?"

"Not just Christmas, for good."

He rubbed at his moustache, deep in thought. She had once hoped he'd come home again, fix the things she broke or had handled badly, but he had his own problems. His wife had been controlling and his home life a mess. He hadn't come. She knew they divorced last year, but she had thought he rented an apartment close to them so he could share custody of the boys.

"Everything came together all at once. My lawyer arranged for Cal and Ry to live with me this summer while the custody hearings finish up. Judith has agreed to letting me have full custody of the boys, and she will get them two weeks at Christmas. That seemed to suit her plans, so once we can get it okayed through the courts, the boys will come here to live with me. I want us to build a life here, specifically on the far side of the river. So, sis, I need you to sign off on your share of the inheritance, one way or the other, so I can get started clearing a place to put a house."

Dread well warranted. She sighed. "You know I'm not ready

to deal with the house. I told you the last time you mentioned it... if you want it, take it. You and the boys could live there."

Lana lived in a tidy apartment building right off the main street in town. It was small, manageable, and it was walking distance to her office. And she'd be moving in a year or two wherever her career took her. There was so much more to life outside Riverbend Falls. She didn't know what, but knew it was out there.

There was a method, a way to do this right. She had been building her reputation globally and had several viable job offers, but nothing that was better than what she was doing. The right thing would come along. She wasn't ready yet, but soon enough, she'd take on the world.

"Do you have a boyfriend? You need someone in your life."

The image of a raven-haired man with bedroom blue eyes, generous lips, and strong sexy hands hijacked her brain. Boy, she was going to stop indulging so heavily in the bodice rippers. She was curtsying and daydreaming like a poorly written heroine.

She shook her head, aggravated. "That's personal."

"Well, I'm your brother, I get to know."

Lana stuck her tongue out at him. "I have no need of a man. I am doing a pretty fine job on my own, if I might say so. Besides, I still think our family is jinxed. Stone marriage's end in divorce or... death."

She believed her relationships were to be intertwined with doom, having witnessed firsthand two instances of many in their family history.

"There's no jinx, Lana. Your problem is you're hardheaded, unyielding, and bossy. Other than that, a peach of a girl." Tad chuckled.

Lana leaned over her champagne. "I work a lot of long hours and I'm not exactly an old maid. I know what I want out of life. One day, I'll break away from here like everyone else." A slow burn was building in her chest. "Once I've conquered the advertising world, I'll retire early. If I do really well, I think I might just buy a little villa in Italy. I'll get a dog, grow a garden, have a swing that squeaks in the wind on the front porch. Bookshelves everywhere. I have a plan. And my plan doesn't include a man." She gave him the haughty look, daring him to boss her around now, after she survived this long solo.

"Whoa, sis, relax. Just needed to know what your living situation is at the moment." Tad held up his hands apologetically. "I have an ulterior motive."

"I'm not surprised," mumbled Lana. She sipped her champagne and tamped down her emotion. She was just fired up because her insides were still warm from being manhandled earlier. "So, what's your ulterior motive?"

"Yeah, so I'm going to put a house roughly across from the old house place. In order to cover the costs and keep paying my custody lawyer, I am going to sell the twelve riverfront acres that border the old mill."

Lana stared at him, astounded. "You're going to sell your land?"

"Just by the dam where it butts up against the Wilcox campground. Really just moving the property line. I'll make more than enough to get a fresh start for the boys and I, only…" He picked up a letter sized manila envelope she hadn't noticed and pushed it across the table. "Peabody said all we need is your signature to accept the terms of Dad's estate, then we both get our full inheritance."

Chapter 2

"In with the copy of the documents, Peabody said there was a cash offer from my buyer for your share." Tad pushed his hand through his hair and smiled like he wasn't wrecking her world. "You don't have to do anything but accept you own it. I wonder, though, if you aren't going to live in the old homestead, why don't you look at this guy's offer?"

"Hold on." Lana closed her eyes, pushing her fingertips together fiercely, breathing, contracting, breathing. Her brother seemed surprised at her reaction, but she had issues, and wasn't in the mood to deal with them, or him, if that's what he was here about. She snaked the envelope off the table, folded it in half, and shoved it into her clutch. She would deal with the emotions her childhood home stirred in her later. Tomorrow, tomorrow was another day. Breathe.

"I'm not ready to deal with it yet, Tad. I just, well, I'll get it handled, though. You know, when the car plowed into that tree, they were fighting over me. When I think of the house, I think of all we lost. It's my fault. I was so impulsive then…" Lana trailed off, distant. Then she took the last swallow of her drink. "You can do whatever you need to with your share, of course, and I'll do whatever I can to help, including my signature, but it's all I can do to think of it, so I shan't, until tomorrow, okay?"

Tad gave her hand a brotherly pat. "You can't blame yourself. It was an accident. Sometimes things just happen. We can let it go for now, but I want you to consider what is best for you. You need to move past that season in your life, little sister. Just think about it. The Mill is part of this town's heritage, and I know you don't want to let that part fade away. It means something to our neighbors here, to us, and it meant something to our folks."

"I have moved forward," insisted Lana, tears blurring her eyes. She wouldn't let them fall, even if he was calling out her emotional nemesis. She'd been running a long time…

"Then you need to realize all the things in your plan," he emphasized the last word, "are right here in Riverbend Falls, where you belong. Step out of the past and make yourself a future."

"I don't know what the future holds and frankly, I don't want to talk about it anymore tonight. I'm homeward bound. It's been a day." Lana gathered up the bag that held what may as well be a poisonous snake in an envelope and stood. Tad was still looking at her like there was more. "What?"

"I wondered if you would mind if I hung around a few days while I get things lined out… since you don't have a steady boyfriend, I won't be getting in your way."

"When you say hang around, do you specifically mean my apartment?" Lana asked.

Tad looked embarrassed. "Yeah. Or I could rent a room at the Inn."

"No problem." Lana waved him along. "But I'm organized, and I like it that way. I can lend you the couch for a few days, though. You can cook. My grilled cheese sandwiches haven't really improved," Lana joked halfheartedly, letting him off the hook. She didn't want to fight, and she was tired of her cooking.

"I'll keep my caveman tendencies to a minimum and be out of your hair as soon as we get a few loose ends tied up, a week or two at the most… thanks, little sister."

Leaving was painless, and as she unlocked the outer door to her small apartment building, she was grateful the evening was over, lightheaded by all the emotional commotion. After setting Tad up with bedding, she left him flipping through all three channels on her ancient television set. She went to her room to lie down and tried to sleep, but her mind wouldn't relax, not with taut muscles and blue eyes crowding her thoughts. She thought about her book, but she needed to resist romantic notions for the moment.

She could see him as if she were staring into a snapshot. She'd never been so perfectly aware of someone. Self-consciously, she touched her fingers lightly to the long narrow scar on her right jaw line. It was her reminder from the accident, bad things happened when she lost control.

Her fingertips moved to her lips, and her stomach fluttered with longing. She thought of the power that had spread through her, stirring her in that moment when their lips had touched and lingered. She had wanted. With a sigh of frustration, she pushed her quilt aside, grabbed earbuds, ready for some loud classical, and bopped over to her treadmill, seeking exhaustion. She ran. Perhaps she would sleep untroubled if she ran long enough.

Shadows ghosted eerily through the trees in the moonlight, the old station wagon's headlights slicing through the night. Lana was in the backseat, ashamed as her parents fought over her. Seventeen—she tried to speak—to beg Dad to stop yelling at Mom, but she couldn't talk. She was sick. Fear gripped her; the familiar icy ball growing in the pit of her stomach. She wanted to focus, but everything was slow and blurry. Angry yelling and indignant shouting. Dad was tired of Lana doing as she pleased, Mom indulged her too much. Sheriff Tate had found them partying again, hauled all three of the best friends to jail to make a point. The girls had been thick as thieves.

"Can't be trusted! Drugs, Betty! A pothead, my daughter!" The derisive words slapped at Lana as she tried to speak. It wasn't as bad as it seemed. She was careful, just a few hits off a joint on special occasions. Perhaps they had emptied the wine bottle Jaime had snitched, but… but she could only whimper pitifully. The bright lights careened out of nowhere. Her dad was looking at her mom, and Lana finally cried out, too late.

"Daddy, look out!"

The car jerked out of the path of the oncoming truck, rounded the curve, and careened off the road into the large old oak. The tree stood solid. In slow motion, her cheek banged into the headrest just as her mom's head smashed the dash. There was so much blood... Lana couldn't reach her. She couldn't wake her dad. The truck had driven on. She had to get help. She climbed out of the car and ran toward town, running, running, running for help. She was all alone in the moon's shadow when the darkness of death came to take her hand...

Lana sat up gasping for breath as she had nearly every night for the past month. It was always worse in the months leading up to the anniversary of their death on New Year's Eve... Oh, she had to get some sleep!

All of that was behind her now. Her parents were dead, and it was too late for sorries. She wouldn't open that cursed envelope. The estate had not been handled because she hadn't wanted to accept the finality of it all. Her parents had provided a trust which essentially took care of itself until she and her brother were ready, so she just put the whole affair out of her mind. She'd delayed lawyer meetings over the years, avoiding Peabody in town until he eventually stopped contacting her about it. She had simply started over, not returning to the emptiness her parents left behind.

If Tad needed her complicity to help him fight for custody of his children, she would toughen up. She realized tears were pouring down her cheeks and lay back down on the bed and began a slow series of stretches, beginning with her toes. It calmed her marginally. Tomorrow. Tomorrow was another day. She fell back into a dreamless sleep.

Lana finished her daybreak run on a path in the park across from her apartment. A solid run strengthened her coping skills, and the control she exercised over her body reassured her she was strong enough for anything she needed to be. She'd made it this far on her own and it was thanks to exercise that she was still sane. She had pushed herself until her muscles ached with a good fatigue. With a quick glance at the time on her pedometer, she noted it was still early. She exhaled slowly, wiping beads of sweat off her face. Her mind cleared completely when she ran, but her body knew to cool down when it was time.

A sense of excitement permeated her last work day before a much-needed few days off for the holiday. As she grabbed bottled water from the fridge, she wondered about her mystery man. He'd been out of place with his suave demeanor and pricy clothes, but he'd been sexy and fresh. She hoped he wouldn't be one of Vivian's regulars, but she'd ask later, after she got her desk cleared... darn! With that envelope from the lawyer occupying her mind and daydreaming about Mr. Freaking Wonderful, she'd forgotten about her 8:00 appointment this morning.

Lana stepped into the shower, trying to extinguish the memory of his sensual hands, the strength he'd lent her in the way he held her, as if she were the woman he'd been looking for. In that few minutes, she tingled with life for the first time in years. He'd overwhelmed her with the tangible sensuality that just wrapped him up like a present, and she hadn't been able to tap her usual defense mechanisms.

The provocative way he drew her in with his eyes... not only did she sense dangerous depths, she wanted to dive deeper. Such overwhelming yum—well, it was new. The steaming shower relaxed the tension in her taut muscles as she soaped her skin, but she couldn't shake the intensity of emotion he generated in her even now.

After showering, Lana looked at her pale face and decided a weekend at a spa might be just the thing. She critically judged the dark circles under her eyes, and thought again about seeing a doctor for some sleeping meds, but yuck. Then she'd be all spun out. Worry about it tomorrow, she thought. Time to get moving now.

She quietly snagged a cup of coffee from her kitchen and slipped into her sunny yellow bathroom to dry and style her hair and put on a touch of make-up. She might be pale, but her mother's smooth skin graced her own complexion and cosmetics weren't necessary, just a bonus.

Wearing her favorite black sweater, an emerald blouse, and

her favorite slacks, she felt the comfort. With a glance in the ornate mirror she'd squeezed into the tiny bathroom, she gave a satisfied nod. Then she grabbed her purse, coat, and a cereal bar from the kitchen and headed out, leaving her brother snoring on her couch.

Garrett rose early, unable to sleep, and discovered an amazing trail behind one of the original guest cabins, the one he would call home. He was still in a foul mood, even when he returned from the run. He needed to cheer up. Happiness was a choice, after all.

It had just been a restless night filled with the lingering scent of honeysuckle and frustration. A fresh pot of coffee welcomed him back into the small kitchenette that still needed groceries, and he filled his tall tumbler with the steaming brew as he promised himself he'd tackle the tasks in good order. Even though things were looking good, he couldn't help being irked at himself. He was letting a woman who clearly hadn't enjoyed his company keep him from sleeping. And he liked his sleep. But he needed to be focused on why he was here.

Culinary school had taught him a lot of things, but very little of it was of use in the time-consuming world of an operational kitchen. He'd taken his first House Manager job at twenty, and on-the-job training took on a new meaning. Operating a restaurant was like an elegant dance, and in those first months, he'd had no moves. Then an old cook took a shine to him, taught him the trick of timing the dance, and he'd started his real training.

A bit of that training had been in women. He grinned and took a swallow of his coffee as he admired the river in the morning's quiet, thinking of the past. Whew, it had been a blast for a while. The classier the jobs got as he rose through the ranks to management, the classier the lady's offer.

Then he discovered women didn't see him. Not once had he met someone who understood that his principles made him, not his bank account. The bank account was a sorrowful replacement for the wonderful grandparents on his mother's side who had since departed earth, leaving him their entire estate when they passed away. No one else could see that. And the lack of communication inevitably led to mind games. Ugh.

After his disastrous near miss with marriage last year, he'd given up women all together, no more settling. If he met a girl, she would be able to carry on a clever conversation. In the meantime, he was going in for all he was worth on a dream he'd devised as a youth after spending a summer here.

Today, he was here, making it happen. He'd taken a leap of faith when he committed to pouring his fortune into this. If he could prove the numbers were there by Memorial Day, an option to buy a franchise for his own restaurant would then round out his all-inclusive resort. Set. For. Life. Doing what he loved, outside, in the most beautiful spot in the world to him.

This meeting could make or break him. This could be a deciding day for his fate in this tight knit community, and his brain was focused on sex.

The lack of focus would not get him where he needed to be. He needed help, and he could buy it. What he didn't have was someone to pave the way with the locals. Get them to accept him. If he couldn't get the popular sentiment of the town, they would make things difficult. And despite how welcome his grandparents made him feel, he was an outsider.

He considered the future as he drove into the quaint hamlet that was a stone's throw from the river. There was less than a half year to get his idea off the ground or he'd lose the contacts he'd made—rich clientele ready to spend money. He'd done a lot of leg work already, several comprehensive lists of modifications and improvements and the expenses, but there was a lot of labor to be done yet. So much to be done.

He was working on buying land from Tad Stone to expand the campground, intending to keep the canoe business, add about sixty kayaks, and about half that many river rafts. There were new cabins already being built, but new campsites needed to be carved out, and he needed to expand the existing boat landings both up and down stream.

A unique bar for his guests was exactly what this town

needed. Some action. Stone's sister owned the homestead and the old grain mill. He considered them vital for the tourist draw, and the homestead he hoped to remodel for the bar, but she'd been dodging his lawyer for months, refusing to take his calls. He'd looked at it, and it was perfect. Plainly nobody cared about the place. He couldn't fathom why she wouldn't sell.

It wasn't the only challenge that daunted him. All the money and effort he'd already invested would be worth nothing if he couldn't start booking the cabins and boats. What he needed was marketing, and it didn't come naturally to him.

If this meeting went well, someone from Vivian's office would work for him exclusively to handle that marketing, orchestrate changes, handle media, and hopefully teach him what he needed to know to do it all himself. Most important, and why he offered to pay so much, he'd have someone on his payroll who could make the connections he would need to draw locals. His Pap was right about breaking traditions, upsetting folks. He grinned at himself. Keeping tradition didn't come naturally, either.

Things might move along as fast as he needed them to if that cagey Stone woman would just sell him her buildings adjoining the land he was gaining from her brother. But even if she miraculously signed the papers, it would still be an intense push to be renting cabins and boats by Memorial weekend. But he could do this. It was everything he wanted.

Lana walked to work despite the chill, just a block from her apartment to the wide sidewalk that flanked Pine Tree Road. Boutiques, antique stores, several offices, and the town's two restaurants lined the town's main street. Her wonderful home away from home, Reed Advertising Agency, was at the far end, next door to Ralph's Grocery. Ralph was stocking fruit at his curbside stand, as usual.

"Morning, Ralph," Lana said. Taking a dime from her coat pocket, where she had a dozen. She handed it to him for the apple he sold her every morning.

"Miss Lana, there you are. I saved my prettiest apple for my prettiest girl."

"Thanks, Ralph," Lana said. She smiled warmly at his teasing, knowing Ralph's longtime crush on Vivian was legendary. "You always take such good care of me."

"I hear we can expect a snowstorm tonight."

"It would be so nice to have a big snow for Christmas," she said.

"Well, I think we'll get it, and the almanac predicts it'll be a humdinger." He walked her next door and held the door open for her. "Have a good day now, and don't work too hard."

"You too, Ralph. Try to keep warm."

Lana walked down the short hallway to her modest office and released a deep breath. A peaceful calm she didn't manage anywhere else slipped over her here and she changed from Lana, restless sleeper and hopeless worrier, into Lana, capable and independent businesswoman. In her office, she hung her coat and stashed her purse in a small cabinet under her office plant. She tucked her cereal bar in her top desk drawer to nibble on later, set the shiny red apple on her desktop, then went down the hall to Vivian's office.

Jealousy shot hot through her blood as Lana realized her mystery man was here, Vivian perched enticingly over him.

He looked good again, and very in control. Dadgummit! She prayed her emotions were not showing on her face. She'd insulted him, yelled at him, kissed him... and he was acting barely aware of her. Unfortunately, she was aware of every inch of him. She thought she could smell his breath mint.

"I apologize for the intrusion. I'll come back later." Lana pivoted at the door, but Vivian stalled her.

"No need—you're right on time to be introduced to our client. This is the account I told you about last night, Lana. Garrett Wilcox, Lana Stone."

All delicious six foot of him stood to take her unsteady hand, but she danced out of his reach, around the chair. Trying to cover mortification at the idea of working anywhere near this man, she attempted to be polite.

"Mr. Wilcox. I'm sure you will find Reed Agency a valuable

asset. We have a lot of talent housed under our roof."

He recovered his unanswered handshake easily, but he gave her a look. His lips curving into a sexy smile that hinted at secrets.

"I admit to being captivated by your talents, Miss Stone. Vivian was sharing some of your more celebrated ad campaigns, and I've seen some of your work in magazines I enjoy." He dipped his head at her. "I appreciate the hospitality synonymous with your company. It shines through. You're quite talented."

Was he taunting her—daring her to comment on their kiss? Hah, not a chance!

Vivian was glowing, and Lana wanted to crawl under the desk.

So, he wasn't Vivian's date? Had he known who she was last night? A ploy... for what? How could she be so dense? She felt a warm flush creep over her body, which morphed into hot shame. Work for him?

She'd get him lined out on that pretty quick. Her brain was whirling. Viv had been very secretive about this account, but she hadn't been able to hide her excitement.

Lana knew Viv had been working on something that was really important to her. This man was going to be around her office a lot, and based on his behavior last night, he was an infuriating person to be around. Without having kissed him soundly.

Chapter 3

"Lana, we've just been discussing the terms Garrett is seeking and I'm hoping you'll agree to give him what he wants." Vivian smiled innocently, which she was clearly not, then added, "I've agreed the full scope of your skills would be available to him through his start-up period, which is an unusually short time. I feel like his request is unusual, but reasonable. It is a three-month contract for you to work solely on the newly born Riverbend Falls Retreat. You can work with that, can't you, dear?"

"No. What? What on earth would take me three months? I can complete the preliminary work in a week. Two weeks might be necessary if it was a difficult client." Lana glared at Garrett a smidge and flopped down in the chair she'd been using as a shield. "That amount of time is simply unnecessary." Three freaking months. It was insanity. No, she would be insane by the end. He disrupted every one of her calming mechanisms. She glared at Vivian's desk.

"I will pay generously for your backing, Miss Stone," Garrett directed his insinuating comments to her and Lana wished she were anywhere else. "I realize I can't hire you directly. Ms. Reed has threatened my hide if I tried, but I want you to teach me everything you're doing, so I don't need to steal you. I figure it'll take me roughly three months following your moves close enough for me to keep the media running afterward. I prefer to be thoroughly involved in each phase of development, including the work you often would do alone or after you leave the job site. We should put our heads together often and share ideas."

Lana looked at him sharply. Surely that last comment wasn't even veiled, but she saw no evidence of anything less than professional in his expression. Realizing she was slumping like a ranch hand, she straightened primly in her chair, tugging at her sweater. Man, it was hot. Someone must have kicked the heat way up. He was still talking.

"… provide an ample expense account and cover all your costs. There is a generous bonus for this project if I am satisfied with the end product, which I suspect I will be, but I'm going to expect you to pitch in wherever you're needed these next few months. Vivian assured me you were up to the challenge."

"I prefer to work alone," she told him. "Vivian." She felt a frown cementing into her face, and she fought the urge to press her fingertips together. This was going to be a disaster. Already she couldn't keep her eyes off his mouth. What the heck was wrong with her? Where was Lana, the polished businesswoman? "I think it might be better to reassign this to Rosemary," she said. She turned to Garrett, "I really don't play well with others," she pretended to be apologetic, but she hoped he could see through her veiled ruse and just go away.

"Nonsense," said Vivian. "This is—"

"No one else will do. I want you." His gaze held heat. "If you're free now, we could go out to the campground and I could prove to you how fabulous my ideas are."

His lips curved into a challenging smile and his blue eyes flickered with longing so briefly Lana wondered if she'd imagined it, wished for it. "Mr. Wilcox…" she began, and he interrupted.

Vivian clearly looked satisfied, and Lana could tell she was all about this. She would be no help.

"Please, call me Garrett." He stood up then and Lana's stomach flip-flopped as she looked up at him, his broad chest towering over her.

"I have other clients—"

Vivian interrupted her. "We'll have Rosemary handle your clients. She's at least familiar with what we have coming up. I think it would be good for her to jump out there." Vivian gave Lana the indulgent smile she saved for her "you need a man," campaign, and Lana knew she was sunk. Vivian was thoroughly enjoying her discomfort. "This will be good for your career, too. Don't worry, Lana, you can handle this."

She glared at Vivian. Of course, she could handle this. She just didn't want to. Who was this guy single-handedly upending her ordered life?

"I'm sure you kids want to get started so, out you go." Vivian waved her hand in dismissal as she took her seat behind her desk.

Lana stood up to escape the room and gave Vivian a lethal look over her shoulder that was ignored completely.

"Look, let's just step into the conference room, perhaps later..."

"Your office, then. I have some ideas and we can look over my notes." Garrett walked to her doorway and stopped, allowing her to enter first. "Your office has a good earthy feel about it. I noticed when Vivian gave me the tour this morning. I'd like you to recreate a similar ambiance in the campground office."

Moving around her desk to her leather chair, the one real luxury in the office, she covered her surprise. It was a pretty eclectic office, and she had designed it herself. He was simply trying to win her over with flattery. She would cope with this, but she didn't have to be a pushover. If she could stomach the arrangement temporarily, she'd think of a way out of working too closely with the man. Distance was key.

"I'm in advertising, not interior design. I'd be happy to look. In your prospectus, I can include design suggestions regarding the advertising benefits that can be tapped by putting logos on the amenities and into your lobbies, but—"

"We have several major business infrastructures to update in three months. I'll be tied to the campground, so I'll need you there, working your magic entirely from the campground offices. Sell my dream for me. The total package, that's what I want." He had settled back into one of the handmade wooden chairs across from her desk, and he looked perfectly serious.

"From your office? No way. I... explain to me why that could be necessary?"

"To reach out to new clientele while maintaining the rapport built with my grandparents' more seasoned guests. Also, to take advantage of the local artisans by courting their business and marketing their wares with flare. I want your opinion and experience so I can manage it all. You'll also have to do a lot of legwork for me. I don't have a team player, and I need one. I also want your help to hire the right people. This as well as the promotional work. I'll need you close."

"My opinion? Legwork?" Lana stared at Garrett in surprise. He was hiring her as a consultant and a *gopher*? Her instinct was to charge down the hall and throttle Vivian. This was not how she worked. Garrett was talking again.

"We'll build on my family's heritage and yours too, if you are willing. I hired you, Miss Stone... Lana, if I may, to help me steer Riverbend Falls Retreat into unchartered territories. With your help, not only will I fulfill my dreams, but other businesses in town will grow more prosperous. It's win-win."

"No, you may not, Mr. Wilcox." Lana stared at him, trying to regain her focus. His mouth was... He was making her uncomfortable. She had a bad feeling about what was coming next. She felt dizzy again. He was sitting so close, despite the desk between them. Her modest office felt cramped. Hot. What was wrong with her? Had she caught the flu?

"What? May not what?"

Then he looked at her with those same hungry eyes he'd devoured her with on the dance floor last night, then in her dreams, and now. Despite his good behavior, he was thinking about that kiss!

"May not... call me Lana. No. Miss Stone will do, Mr. Wilcox. Your behavior—my behavior—last night was quite inexcusable, and very inappropriate since we're to be... coworkers." She paused, tugged at her hair, pushing the locks from her neck. It was so very hot.

"That was just a dance to me, mister, and I don't yet know that I like you. However, I will help you. For the obscene amount of money you're paying me to assist," she narrowed her eyes at him slightly, "how could I refuse? You definitely bear looking after if you aren't planning to make a fool of yourself in this town, charging in, kissing everybody. Anyway. What is this dream of yours?"

He grinned at her, straight white teeth flashing. "Doing a job I love, equivalent to eternal retirement for me. I'm starting with Pap and Gran's campground and planning an overhaul. My resort will become synonymous with river fun for all walks of life; rich, poor, middle class, happy, horny, drunk, a little wild, all of them river people. I want classy but affordable, with some luxury packages for my high-end guests. These are tough times and all people need fun. I can give them that. More boats, more accessibility... My resort, now that your brother is selling me that brief stretch of land between your Mill and my campground will be a popular playground for all... lovers, families, friends. New traditions will start in Riverbend Falls, and we'll be part of them."

His eyes were keen, far seeing, and Lana found herself caught up by his excitement... then he crashed her into the wall of bad dreams. He just kept talking. "The history of the Mill is rich in traditions just begging to be rehabilitated. Are you really going to let it fade away?" He leaned back casually and slid his hands behind his head, interlocking his fingers. "If you'll work for me for money when you so obviously don't want to be friends, why won't you sell to me for money? Not enough?"

She started choking on her response and Garrett popped to his feet, leaning over so close she felt the warmth of his wintergreen-scented breath. "Are you all right? Can I get you something?"

Lana stood abruptly, almost bumping foreheads with him. She stepped back. "Seriously, you weird me out, man. I'm fine. The Mill is my private business for now. If I change my mind, maybe, maybe, I'll let you know how much money I would accept for my home."

"So an early dinner, then? I'll meet you here at four?"

"What? No, I can't..." Home. She'd called it home. That bore thought, later.

"Sure you can," he interrupted smoothly. "I'll give you a little time to gather yourself and prepare to be uprooted temporarily. It's obvious I caught you off guard here, and I need you to be at your best. I'll pick you up later and we can review my ideas. I'll leave them with you if you want to peruse them, but remember, I want to be a part of the full process. We'll discuss it over dinner. I saw a café up the street."

"No, I mean..." He was so straight and tall, Lana remembered how solid his arms felt. Hmmm. "I mean, later, the cafe at six. I'll meet you there. Mr. Wilcox, don't forget, this is purely business. No kissing!" She sat back down, then added sweetly, "And you'll be on the clock."

He leaned against her desk again, hair arrogantly falling into bedroom blue eyes, and *winked* at her. When did her desk shrink? "Until then, river goddess." Then he was gone.

Lana regarded Wilcox's daunting file. Having worked through lunch, she crunched into her sweet red apple and barely noticed its flavor, preoccupied. She wasn't emotionally equipped to deal with this. It was impossible.

She looked at the neat stacks of paper on her desk covered with post-it notes, instructions printed in her neat handwriting. There was little else to do until April. Picking up the unopened file, she realized that in the space of 24 hours, what was supposed to be a four-day holiday weekend had turned into a 90-day sentence of servitude outside her comfort zone. She walked to Vivian's office and popped the door open as Vivian waved at her through the glass.

"Well?" Vivian asked. "He's attractive, isn't he?"

"I couldn't say," Lana said. "This is so uncool, Vivian. You're railroading me." She tried to still her trembling hands by fisting them at her hips, hoping Vivian would give up.

"Just noting the obvious, darling." Vivian said, eyeing Lana shrewdly. "So, will you do the job? He needs help, guidance at least, or this town will lose a chance at what could be a tremendous asset for us here in town if he succeeds. I want our best person on point for this. That's you. I already assured the council that he hired us and you are assisting."

"I just..." She came in and sat in her chair from earlier.

Vivian interrupted. "Can you help him transform a family campground into a luxury resort, market it successfully, and keep him out of trouble here in town? Admit it, it sounds exciting. If I was a few years younger..." Vivian stretched her arms over her head and laughed. "But I'm not, and it would be a fun change of pace for you. Transfer a few accounts and embrace the challenge, my dear."

"Not much to transfer." Lana shrugged jerkily, then chastised herself. This was no reason to disrespect her mentor. Lana would just figure out a way to do what was being asked of her. She would handle Kat's business from her apartment since they mostly traded services, anyway. Some of her clients might complain a little, but once Rosemary turned on her southern grits charm, they'd be thrilled. She was talented and had a flair of her own.

But to ice her hard won clientele for months to placate a playboy? She wouldn't do it. She couldn't work side by side with him. He made her brain scat. Then what good would she be?! But this was plainly important to Viv...

"I finished the bulk of my first quarter assignments. I left mock-ups of the spring posters for Renee's Boutique on my desk. And the new layout for the grocery store flyer you asked for is in your email. I think Ralph will really like the layout you suggested. I thought you might want to give it to him. I left a stack of post-it's on some files for Rosemary. If you think she wouldn't mind chasing down any stray details and following up if need be?"

"I think she will be happy, too. I'll ask her when she gets back, but I'm pretty certain."

Vivian nodded at her, and Lana sensed her approval. She couldn't promise she could do this, though.

"I haven't actually decided if I want to do this or not, but I will give it a Girl Scout try, because I love you, and you never ask me for anything. Unless you're nagging me to get a date, and that is not what this is." She did a few finger flexes while she ordered her thoughts. There she was, the competent businesswoman. "I will do my best on this job." Quickly.

She wouldn't let a few gooey feelings and a little accidental kissing ruin her reputation. She would do the job well. Then move on. Another win.

"Good. So, are you headed out?" Vivian asked, glancing at the files on her own desk. "Want to grab a late lunch?"

"No, Garrett and I are planning to brainstorm over dinner. I'm going to meet him at six. I suppose I'll put together a prospectus based on this." She glared at the folder she'd laid beside her. "I've cleared my projects, so I'm going to take this one and head home, I guess." Then she brightened.

"I'll pray for a snowstorm. Ralph said it would snow tonight, and he's right more often than the weatherman! Maybe there will be snow for Christmas, starting tonight, and the roads would be slick so..." She glanced at Vivian and interrupted herself, chagrined. "A smidge too much drama?" she asked. "Rosemary will handle anything that comes up, I guess. Three months, Viv?"

"You and Garrett are having dinner tonight?" Vivian asked, *that* smile playing at the corner of her lips. "Hah! Your meeting got comfortable. I knew you'd like him. And there was chemistry between you two already."

Lana flushed. Oh yeah. Chemistry, good word. Like a volcanic science experiment. If Viv hadn't heard the gossip from the dance, Lana wasn't mentioning they'd already met. Lana found renewed hope that no one else noticed the spooning and kissing... Oh, good grief.

"Please get that ridiculous matchmaking look off your face, Viv. This is purely business."

"No, really." Vivian loved the game, smoothly ignoring Lana's glare. "This will be good for your career, sweetie."

She came around her cherry wood desk and propped herself

on the corner. After a moment, she leaned down to give Lana a firm hug, holding tight before leaning back on her desk.

"Seriously, Lana, you could have been running your own business these past few years, but because I hope you'll stay right here in Riverbend Falls, spreading your sunshine, I'm not going to tell you how great you are, how far you could go in this world. Since you came to me for a job when you were seventeen, I've never stopped being proud of you, as your boss and your friend. I believe you can accomplish anything you want, but you must be open to opportunities when they come your way. Remember that. Now go on, get out of here and have a Merry Christmas. Go on before I get all teary-eyed and my mascara runs."

Lana softened, her heart melting. "Oh, Viv, you know I couldn't have made it without you. I just can't believe I won't be here every day. I'll be working in some strange office with strange everything... until March! I thought when I left this office I would go to New York or something, not go to work for an overgrown boy on his fantasy campground."

She looked around the room she knew so well. Magazine covers and awards plastered the walls, some of them Lana's own work or awards for it. How many times she'd shared her lonely tears with Viv in this office.

"You better bet I'll be around, so be sure no one runs off my clients while I'm assisting the impetuous Mr. Wilcox." She stood. "Merry Christmas, my friend." She squeezed Vivian in another tight hug and wondered just how screwed she was.

He rattled her. She wanted to maintain formality. It was a shield that worked! As she walked down her familiar path for the last time for a while, having warned Ralph she'd be out of the office but in for groceries on Fridays, Lana wrestled with confusion.

Her comfort zone had been obliterated, first her brother, then her body, now her office. Lana liked neat and organized, not tumultuous and unplanned. There was, however, no denying the surge of pleasure she felt when he winked at her, and his sassy flattery tickled her plum to her toes.

Tad left a note on the glass coffee table saying he'd be back late. He was attending the auction at the cattle barn. She sat in her living room on the fluffy gray carpet and opened his folder. She would focus, and fulfill her responsibilities to Vivian, her responsibility to represent the agency in the best possible light, and now her responsibility to help Garrett Wilcox build a resort without destroying the peace in her town.

She was impressed with his planning. Despite his imprudent ideas, his business model was simple, and while charts and graphs weren't one of his strengths, he'd roughed out all the figures. It was full of hand-written notes, some projected profit-and-loss sheets, and a few fliers from other successful companies. It was going to cost a small fortune to build what he was planning—and be disruptive.

No wonder Vivian was worried about the council. By the time summer rolled around, if he achieved even half his goals, Riverbend Falls would crawl with tourists well supplied with alcohol and plenty of things to spend money on. She'd have to help the locals see the revenue it would bring. Tourists would shop in their stores; buy their jams, jellies, and fresh produce. It seemed he had contracted local construction crews to build the cabins he was planting on the riverbank where she'd played as a girl…

Lana sat back, a memory bubble bursting. His haunting blue eyes. She *had* seen them before. The summer she was ten. Tad just turned fourteen, and finally they could play at the river without supervision. Tad fished—Tad always fished—and he would walk upstream, leaving her to dance and play mermaid. She held court for her imaginary friends, talking to her subjects, then one day she realized she had a real audience. The boy came every day for two weeks and played a hunting game in the brush or something. He never asked her to play. Sometimes she watched him, though, when he wasn't watching her with those bright blue eyes.

He never returned and soon she replaced her imaginary friends with her best friends. Jaime's family had moved to Riverbend Falls, and Lana and Kat quickly accepted her. The three became inseparable. Then the winter of their senior year, a New Year's party changed everything...

Enough. She'd worry about it tomorrow.

So, what did she know about this guy, anyway? He was Jasper and Emily's grandson. They often boasted about their successful chef grandson when she saw them at the cafe, and Emily loved to share the comical kitchen tales he emailed her. She knew Jasper and Emily had a retirement party a few months ago back at the close of the season, but she hadn't gone. It never occurred to her to ask what was happening to the campground, because she never went there anymore.

The only way there was straight past her parents' house.

Pulling her knees up, she rested her head on them. She could tap hidden reserves. Find enough courage to face the old homestead issue so she could help Tad. Or she could dig deep and agree to work outside her comfort zone to create a business that was bound to change the dynamic of her town, a dynamic she didn't know she would like. It would be... disorderly.

A surety that she could be easily overwhelmed and her world would crash down on her was growing. She feared she might need every tool in her arsenal to fight her impractical attraction to the unrelenting charm being heaped on her by Garrett Wilcox.

This was her jam, though, and she almost convinced herself if she was diligent, she could cut short the time she was supposed to spend with him. She gave a last flustered look at the antique clock on the wall. Since it was already after five, she'd have to hurry and get ready. Though getting dressed up wasn't the plan.

She glanced out her big bay window and realized fat snowflakes were floating down and had been for some time. A winter white coat draped the landscape, putting her to mind of the dance she'd shared with Garrett last night. Latching on to the weather as an excuse not to meet him for dinner, she entered the cell number Garrett—Mr. Wilcox left her and sent him a text.

"Considering the weather, I'd like to reschedule our meeting for tomorrow, if you aren't otherwise obligated."

There. She felt a little sheepish for being too chicken to call, texting was a little tacky, but that's what assistants do, right? By tomorrow, she would have herself pulled together, and have enough mock up work to skimp on the alone time. He wouldn't like it, probably, but she did not like having to work within any proximity to G… him.

She tossed her phone on the coffee table, feeling like she'd won a minor battle.

An hour and ten minutes later, Lana looked up from the pages of ideas and figures she'd been slowly digesting. There was a knock at her door. Hmmm… She'd told Tad to make himself comfortable, but it was nice that he would be polite. She opened the door, intending to ask him if he brought a cow home with him. It was not Tad.

Chapter 4

"Hiya, babe." Garrett stood in her doorway. "Can I come in?"

"How the heck...? How... how did you know where I live?" Lana wanted to disappear through the floor. He looked good in khaki slacks and his brown blazer had a sweet sprinkling of melting snow on the shoulders. He smelled like... fries. How could he come here? Ohhh, not good.

"I brought burgers and beers."

He lifted two white bags with grease spots soaking through and carried a brown paper sack in his other hand. He watched her watch him for a second and his eyebrows curved up, daring her. Her response to his presence was to run. He was breaking into her shell uninvited, and he was too... She'd already agreed to work for him. What else could he want from her? She just stared.

"You're not actually that hard to track down. The guys at the cafe were pretty helpful." He motioned he couldn't get past her unless she invited him in, and she stared, debating. "There aren't many apartment buildings here on the square, and I figure a girl has to eat, blizzard or no. Did I mention the weather in this town is crazy? It was sixty degrees yesterday."

Lana couldn't resist a small smile, flattered he would go to any trouble after she pointedly blew him off. She moved back, allowing him in. "I left you a text asking to reschedule. Did you get it?" She tried to play it cool.

"Yeah, but I'm 'otherwise obligated' and didn't want to reschedule. I got you the works; they said that's how you like your burgers. Extra fries too. Do you always get the king size?" He gave her an appraising look, and Lana felt very vulnerable in her pajama bottoms. "Amazing you're so skinny."

"I'm not skinny!" She hesitated, following him into her shrinking living room. He sat on her couch, took an opener out of his pocket, and opened two Coronas. Hmph. "I guess, since you're here, I might as well have one of those, but," Lana eyed him distrustfully, accepting the beer he'd opened for her, "before you hand me any of that delicious smelling food, Mr. Wilcox, I want to be clear. What happened last night was a fluke. Now we are conducting a business arrangement. I know we agreed already, but I would consider pursuing anything else very unprofessional, and outside our best interests. Don't forget."

"I have a feeling, Miss Stone, I won't be able to forget. Do you want plates?"

"Yeah." Lana was still wondering how, with all her careful evasions, this handsome, impulsive man was moving into her organized kitchenette, carrying a bag of fries. She followed him. "Extra fries, huh? Good, I'm hungry."

"Me too." The look he gave her before reaching into a cabinet to find two plates left her wondering at what he was agreeing to being hungry for. When he reached past her to the microwave for extra napkins, his arm brushed hers, and her stomach fluttered with desires that felt too tingly and good for her to regret them. This was bad. How was she to manage when, every time they were close, she went gooey? Ugh!

"I don't think it's a good idea for you to be here, Mr. Wilcox. Is this necessary…" She trailed off, looking at him hopefully, then cursed herself. She didn't want him to leave at all. But he had tightened up. His blue eyes were all business, and despite being pushy and demanding, he behaved like a gentleman. There was not even a hint of fiery desire in his eyes. It was awful.

When Lana had opened the door, Garrett knew he had shaken her up again. Determined to see her relax, he felt like he was succeeding a little at a time, but he wasn't really a patient guy. He wanted to melt her frosty barriers, and though he knew she wouldn't appreciate it, he wanted to feel her heart-shaped lips pressed against his again. It was all he could think about.

"Is this absolutely necessary...?" She had asked, and for him, it seemed to be. This woman presented him with a dilemma. Destiny assured they would meet. He could easily admit to himself that since his failed engagement, women were just a hassle—until now.

Somehow, with no encouragement, she left him feeling edgy, wanting to be with her. He needed her to maintain the professionalism she was using as a shield. The fact he wanted her house and the Mill property for himself was only complicating things further. Things would have been simpler had she accepted his offer before he arrived. Too bad his libido didn't agree with his business sense; he wanted her, and he was afraid he had it bad.

"Lana, call me Garrett, won't you? We're going to be working closely, so you might as well try to relax."

"I... fine. Garrett."

He eyeballed her fuzzy green pajamas with dancing frogs frolicking on them and smiled. How would he settle down in a town where people put pajamas on before ten? He was going to have to shake things up this summer. Lana bent over in the doorway to pick up a paper napkin that dropped off the empty plates on her way to the kitchen. She'd polished off the fries, hers and his, and as Garrett watched her, he wondered how she kept such a tight figure. He wanted very much to see more of her, in and out of the pajamas.

She called out from the kitchen, where he could hear water running. "Peruse the plans I've been putting together there on the coffee table."

He leaned in, irritated. She wasn't supposed to work without him. If he was going to manage everything on his own after their contract expired, he needed to follow everything she was doing. She came back into the living room, rubbing a honeysuckle smelling lotion on her hands. She smiled, and the sunshine thawed the iceberg she had positioned between them.

Well, great. That was going to be short-lived.

"You were supposed to look over what I want from you, Lana. Maybe make a few notes, not go off on your own deciding what you think should be. We do this my way. You work for me, and you show me how you do what you do. That's what it says in the contract you signed."

"I... what?" She gave him a blank look.

"You don't want to work with me?" He asked, stepping closer to her.

"I... well, I just don't want..."

"It's already complicated, Lana." He interrupted, moving closer as he read the desire in her eyes. She was fighting herself, but she was interested. And he wanted her.

"How did you know...?"

"It's written all over your face. You can't categorize and label what's already happened, what's going to happen between us, and you don't like it one bit."

She stared at him, saying nothing, but gave herself away as she looked at his lips, her tongue delicately sneaking out to touch her own lips.

"I'm going to kiss you again," Garrett said, whispering softly as he leaned down, tipping her chin up to taste her lips.

It was not a gentle continuation of what had begun the night before. The kiss kindled instant desire, and he almost ended it before it burned either of them, then Lana's arms went around his neck, pulling him into her heat, and the fire built between them as they stroked hands in hair and their tongues tasted and devoured. She was literally a perfect fit in his arms, for his mouth, and his body was insisting he find out if they matched as perfectly in bed.

Garrett nipped at Lana's bottom lip tenderly and broke away from her.

Oh, it was complicated all right.

He walked to the window and stared out silently for a minute, then returned to the coffee table and gestured at her notes. The pages were divided by department, color coded, and annotated.

"I can see you're becoming familiar with what I want, but I can't help notice you are pointedly not acknowledging I need your property for my plans. If you'd just accept my offer, it would make you rich. Why the hesitation? It's badly in need of restoration, and I can afford to do that. It's perfect for my needs."

"You don't need much, do you?" Lana said, quiet as she gently tapped her lips, her finger wandering over them before moving to the little battle scar on her cheek. "How can you kiss me like that then want to discuss business?! The most unpleasant business."

"It doesn't have to be unpleasant." He kept his tone mild, but he needed the already established buildings for his expansion. He needed lodges for the corporate parties, the Mill itself would be an incredible draw, and when he owned it, he would capitalize on that... but he couldn't push her to sell what had been in her family for generations, for what his Pap recently referred to as a tourist trap! But it would be so much more when he was done with it.

She sighed, and sat down, deflated, on her couch. "I know it's not fair. The mill itself was such an important part of Riverbend Falls's heritage. Did you know people used to come in wagons from miles around to have corn and wheat milled?"

She didn't look up at him, just started a story he had known, though maybe not understood. This was *her* heritage.

"Early farmers settled the town, including my great grandparents, who stayed on after the harvest season. Businesses sprang up—a cotton gin, a blacksmith shop, a general store—people spent money when they came in, celebrating good harvests, perhaps to share or trade with those who hadn't done so well. I always had a notion of wanting to share that part of history back to the town. When my folks died, I left that part of me behind. And I haven't been back."

She glanced at him then, and the depth of pain he saw in her eyes nearly crippled him. He had done this to her. Just charged into her life and caused havoc, like he always seemed to do.

"I really had planned to deal with it later, only I fear later just caught up to me." She stood, and her shields came back in to place as if the poor lost soul he'd just seen had never been. "Is that why you hired me? Did you seek me out to convince me to sell my land to you?"

"I need the best of everything, babe," Garrett said, watching her. "That's why I hired you." She shook her head angrily, and he reassured her. "Look, I didn't know it was you I was hiring. I didn't know you last night at your party." He walked back to the window, looking out over the park across the street. "If I did, it wouldn't have changed anything. What is happening between us, well, you're right. It's complicated, so let's give it a little breathing room." He turned back to her with his best smile. "The snow has stopped. Let's take a walk." Because he needed air or he was going to kiss her again.

"Let's look at this together, then we'll see how we feel." Work with him. She could do this. "I apologize for getting ahead of myself. I found myself caught up in ways to make a few things work better. We can just scratch this, though, and start fresh."

He gave her a hard look, then sighed. "No, let's see what you've got."

She settled across from him on the floor and began laying out a job schedule, that outlined each of the next twelve weeks on several sheets of paper, and his eyes were alight with excitement by the time he got to page two.

Nearly an hour later, almost nine, Lana looked over at her couch where Garrett was sitting back and wondered what was happening to her for about the tenth time. He appeared relaxed and lost in thought as he stared at another page, then jotted down another margin note before looking at her, catching her eyes. They were sitting around her living room, brainstorming and arguing like old friends, and she was having a blast.

On a normal day, she never would have let him through the door. She felt the oddest sensations around him. Perhaps the fanciful poet's notion, "butterflies in her tummy."

Surely the energy coursing through her body when she got

close to Garrett was a reaction to her non-existent sex life. She was a woman. Her body would react to the charm of enchantment Garrett was working on her. And he was a fine specimen of a man. She had her work cut out for her.

It would be better if his attention didn't make her feel so special. Handsome men sometimes offered her dinner. Just because they were usually married, old, or boring didn't matter. Garrett appeared to be none of those things, and he was likely no stranger to getting what he wanted from a woman.

He wanted something from her. Probably more than one something, she thought wryly, trying to decide which prospect was more unsettling.

He had had his feet lazily crossed at the ankles, stretching out in front of him. She remained lotus style on the carpet, not trusting herself to sit up on the couch next to him when he asked about some detail, something she'd written on his notes. She already felt way too comfortable with this man who disrupted every aspect of her precise lifestyle. He remained the perfect gentleman. It was time to get rid of him.

She could tell him she was tired. It was late. Tomorrow was Christmas Eve. He certainly couldn't be planning to hang out much longer. Tad would be back soon, hopefully.

They spoke at once, laughed, then started again at the same time. Garrett just chuckled, pulling out of his slouch and stretching his fantastic arms over his head.

"You first."

Lana smiled. "I was going to offer to walk you out."

"Let's take a short walk first, stretch our legs for a few minutes."

Lana hesitated, then rolled with it. "Some fresh air before we go to bed is probably a good idea."

Not meaning to insinuate 'we' and 'bed' was an option. She felt a flush creep into her cheeks, but he didn't seem to notice the slip.

"Let me grab some warmer clothes." She disappeared into her bedroom and came back in a colorful warm-up suit pulled over her pajamas and was pulling on a rainbow crocheted hat and mittens. From the coat rack behind the door, Garrett selected the puffy bright green ski jacket Jaime had mailed her last Christmas and held it out for her.

She avoided making eye contact before she turned to slide into it. How could she be wishing to kiss him again? She had to stop herself. Land sakes, she was going to be working with this man. Likely, he had a girlfriend of some sort wherever he came from. Regardless, she had to keep her head in the game—no time for romance in the advertising world unless you were working on a campaign for a lingerie or candy store... If you had an edge, you had to keep it.

Garrett gently lifted a strand of her blond hair that had escaped her ponytail, tucked it behind her ear, then ran a gentle thumb across her lips. The touch seared, leaving her wanting more. "Ready, gorgeous?"

Lana wrestled with herself, determined to chastise his brazen behavior, but knowing she liked it. She was such a hypocrite. She knew full well she'd spent much of the past two days wondering what another kiss would be like. Would it measure up, or was it a fluke? The answer had been, oh yeah, his kisses were Richter scale hot. Hot and crazily intimate.

"If you can keep your hands to yourself, I'm ready." She walked out the door, leaving him to follow.

He was incredible, Lana thought, restraining a smile. His bold moves triggered more of her emotions than she liked, but she would get them under control. She already wished she hadn't agreed to walk with him. She shouldn't allow him to keep surprising her. It was throwing her off balance. She would pack her emotion into the box. She was no amateur at that.

Stepping into the frosty night air, the profound beauty of winter took her breath. Bright moonlight reflected in the glistening snow, and it almost seemed like daylight. The wind had died down, the air was still. About six inches of snow had accumulated, which was unusual for her neck of the woods, and with Christmas lights shining from her neighbor's window, the scene was a dream.

There was warmth between Lana and Garrett that kept the

cold off as they trudged toward the park. Not another soul in sight. Their shoulders touched companionably every few steps. She felt her heart shimmer and was grateful Garrett couldn't see inside her. She'd not met anyone like him, and they had practically nothing in common, but the fire in his kisses explained the liveliness in her step. She really needed to come back to earth.

"So what is it you need from me, Garrett? You aren't paying me a nearly a year's salary for three months just to fetch you coffee, I hope."

"For starters, I need you to help me with some clothes shopping. I noticed few people wore suits for your dance last night, and I haven't much suitable, haha, to work in. You could help me choose some clothes to help me fit in around here."

"Shopping? Garrett, it's going to take a lot more than clothes and that phony twang you've been working on for you to fit in around here." She gave him an appraising look and admitted to herself that he'd look good in a paper sack. "But some more laid-back clothes wouldn't hurt. Yeah, you can probably skip the Armani, though it is nice." Lana leaned down and scooped up some snow in her glove, squeezing it into a snowball before launching it into a drift just ahead. "Even though the campground base is at the river, most of the traffic will still come through town and several of the older folks won't appreciate it if they just see a bunch of drunk idiots running around."

"That's why we are going to give them plenty of places to sleep in my cabins on the river. The crowds may drink and hurrah down at the water, but I figure it won't be too bad through town."

Lana mused thoughtfully… "I think you should consider giving them a place to dress up and go out to dinner on site, too. Maybe a restaurant to balance the bar?"

"Good idea." Garrett gave her a speculative look. "Do you already have plans for tomorrow?"

"Christmas Eve? Not really. Why?"

"Why don't you have a Christmas tree in your apartment?"

Lana looked at him, surprised. "I don't know. I guess I usually do the decorating for the Christmas dance, and by the time I've decorated for the whole town, I guess I'm just... y'know, all decorated out."

"I've always loved Christmas," Garrett said, melancholy in his tone. "My parents—I don't think they've ever been here, so you wouldn't know them—they always spend Christmas at St. Bart's."

"Oh..." Lana got all dreamy. "Jaime told me it's one of the greatest places to be at Christmastime. Anybody who's anybody is there." She gave him what she hoped was an average encouraging smile. She had pictured herself there, with him! Be casual already. "So, is it everything they say?"

"I don't know. I've never been." A brief shadow crossed his features and disappeared. "But I'd rather be right here. Thirty years old and this will be my first real Christmas with the family deal and all. My grandparents are excited. Me too. I bet you're terrific at wrapping presents. Maybe you could help me out?"

She started to decline, frantically wracking her brain for something good when he went on.

"Business, of course, first. I'd like to take you by to visit with my grandfather a bit about our ideas. I could use your help to reassure him." He gave her a wry smile, flashing those straight white teeth. "He might be some of that older crowd who isn't sure about my, well, Pap calls it my 'hostile takeover' of Riverbend Falls." With a mischievous look in his eye, he reached over and took her hand.

"I, I... oh heck, you're gonna run my sanity plum out the door, aren't you?" Lana giggled, her hand warming through her glove, and she didn't want to move it, but she did, reaching down to form another snowball. "I suppose I could help you out, but I'm telling you, you're on the clock, buddy." She tossed the snow in the air and it landed inches in front of Garrett.

"Good, then we'll go by your old house. You can give me a tour and remind me why you don't want me to have it."

Lana turned to him, incredulous. "I just remembered you crashed my apartment tonight because you have plans tomorrow."

Chapter 5

"That is my plan." He'd scooped some snow of his own and was using it to avoid her stare, rubbing his long naked fingers over the orb until it was a perfect circle.

"I don't think..." Splat. Garrett hit her square in the chest of her overcoat, smattering snow across her chest. "Oh, you shouldn't have! You've started war with the snowball queen."

Humor glinted in Garrett's eyes. He knew he was getting under her skin, and she just bet that was part of his plan, too. He popped another one in her direction, hitting her in the arm. "Agh," Lana sputtered, and launched one back at him. Garrett ducked behind a tree as the snowball smacked the bark with a resounding thud.

"You'll have to be faster than that, snowball queen," Garrett taunted as he lobbed another snowball at her legs.

"Oh, you're rotten..." Lana trailed off as she hit him in the chest with a snowball. "There," she said, throwing her arms in the air with delight. The gloating ended as another snowball pegged her leg.

Just as Lana was about to launch a full-scale tactical maneuver, Garrett slipped up next to her. "Truce?"

"Not until we're even." Lana scooped up a large handful of snow and dropped it over his head. She laughed at his surprise while snow drifted down around his ears, piled up on those sexy shoulders. "OK, maybe now we're even enough for a truce."

Garrett put on a wounded look, and she indulged herself, linking her arm through his as they stomped through the snow back to her apartment. He had cheered by the time they arrived. "I don't suppose you would offer a cold, wet man a nightcap in your warm apartment?"

Her heart opened a bit, though not fooled by the charm he laid on so thick. She was a professional. She patted his arm, flashed a sunshiny smile, and angled him toward the black SUV parked in front of her building, the only vehicle on the street she didn't recognize.

"Not gonna happen... I only agree with our business arrangement." Having him in her apartment had not been a good idea. She should have just ventured to the diner in the snow. She shook her head in the negative. Now she would feel him there.

"We'll just figure us out as we go along." He shrugged. "Suits me."

"Garrett, I really can't get involved with anyone at this point in my life, especially not someone I work with... or for, whatever."

He freed his arm, which, despite her words, she was still clinging to. With an ice-cold thumb, he rubbed her cheek, creating heat. Her protest stopped forming. She wanted to go on, but the moment he caressed her, she wanted him more.

"I can't afford to be distracted right now, either. You don't have to be afraid of what's going on between us. I like you, but I don't see why it has to affect our work. Look, I'll see you tomorrow. Be ready by nine. We'll have a big day."

Lana was not sure about this at all. Could things be worse? But she was already having more fun than she had in a long time—as long as she kept everything professional. She would use this job to push right through dealing with the house.

And he just admitted he wasn't looking for a relationship either. That made it safe, right?

"Look, I'm not sure. Don't you have a girlfriend or something that can help you with the personal stuff? I'd rather just stick to the work I'm used to doing, y'know? Advertising copy, charts and posters, press releases..."

"No. I really need your help on a lot of levels, Lana. I'm like a fish out of water here. I've never tried small town life before. I need you."

"I suppose," said Lana, unsure. "But you must be a man of your word. We'll maintain a working relationship, and you have to stop being so bossy and take my advice when I give it to you. And we can't pursue this... whatever it is."

"I'm not bossy. I just know what I want." It seemed to Lana he glazed over giving his word. "I'll see you tomorrow, then?"

"I... yes," she said, her voice a near whisper. Heaven help her. She wanted to taste his kiss one last time, then she would annex this out of her system.

He leaned in close, his warm breath so close to her ear it spun the butterflies in her belly up through her chest. "Dream of me, river goddess." With a sly look, he retreated to his eye candy of a ride and climbed in. A smile and a wave, and he was gone.

No kiss.

Lana stood in the stairwell a minute before catching herself and climbing the short flight to her apartment. So he didn't kiss her. That is what she spent the entire night demanding. What was wrong with her? How could she possibly work with this man when she turned into a ninny near him?

She might have apologized Monday morning for yelling at him at the dance if he had not seemed so pushy, smug. As it was, she had disliked him passionately by the time he left her office. Then when he showed up at her door, spent all that time good naturedly arguing out their ideas, lying around on her furniture and acting as if he belonged, she accidentally wondered what it would be like to have him permanently in her life.

He threw snowballs. His kisses left her mouth numb. His touch left her body humming. The worst part was when he left the room. Her vision cleared and she could focus again, but the atmosphere dimmed.

She had no time for fantasies, knowing she could not throw

her rules aside for a handsome face. It was more than protection for her, it was protection for him, too. Fate was not kind to her, and she wasn't willing to risk anyone else sharing that with her. Until she dealt with the crushing guilt over how her parents died, there was no way to open up enough to let a potent emotion like love into her life.

Once Garrett realized she indulged in toting piles of emotional baggage, and her family had a legacy of doomed relationships, he would not be so interested. But she couldn't just say the words. It would give him insight into her personal life she wasn't willing to share. She *could* stay aloof.

Vivian encouraged her to watch for opportunity. His changes would impact the way of life here. His determination to do everything in three months was ridiculous.

More ridiculous, she was apparently taking the job. This was not an opportunity; it was a catastrophe.

This whole situation mystified her. She could not deny the thrill she felt in his arms. If she let herself remember, she could feel the sizzling imprint his touch had left on her skin. It was downright terrifying.

She would be in his territory now, and knew it would be tough. She wondered if his nearness would continue to influence her self-control. Boy, she hoped not. Whenever she got in one of these funks, one of the girls would work her through it.

Kat had gone to visit her Aunt Lucy for Christmas, but Jaime was always on the other end of the line, no matter where she was or what time it was. Lana picked her phone up from the well-ordered charging station beside her bed, leaned back against the pillows with her legs crossed, and sent the call.

Jaime answered on the second ring, "What's up, girl? Can't sleep?"

Lana rolled her eyes and hit the speakerphone. Her friends knew her so well. "Yes, Doctor J, I'm finding sleep elusive."

"Doctor J. I like that. I could start an advice column instead of running around, making everyone in the restaurant industry hate me. I love to give advice." She laughed, then said seriously,

"I mean it. I love that picture of you hiking last week, but, girl, your body is a shrine. Making the rest of us hotties look lazy. My official prescription… consider skipping the evening torture ritual—er, exercise routine—twice a week."

"Whatever… So, a lot happened this week." Lana leaned back on her bed, arms wrapping around herself. This was what she needed, someone who always cut through the chaff. "So I was at the Christmas dance, wearing a fabulous new dress. I rocked the décor, and I was feeling sassy. It's my only excuse for what happened next."

"Juicy," Jaime said in a singsong voice. "I sense a man."

"Girl, your interest in men never fails. You rival Viv. Yes, a man. It's complicated."

"Uh huh, tell Dr. Jaime what happened. I'm already disappointed cause I can tell by the sound of your voice you didn't get laid."

"I did not. I'm perfectly happy with the state of my love life. It's uncomplicated. You know I like it that way. Anyway, nothing really happened. Just a dance. Two dances, really."

"You mean you were too dreamy to shake him off after the first dance? Oh, this is good." Jaime laughed. "What did he look like? Was he tall? I love tall ones. They just fold you into their arms. It's so sexy. I can already tell he was dark and handsome. No pretty boy would sway you from your dedication to celibate thoughts."

"Jaime, quit harassing me. I'm not telling you what he looked like. You're having too much fun fantasizing about it. I will tell you, though, he had muscular arms, and I've never felt safer. And he was a great kisser."

"I thought you said you only danced," Jaime practically squealed.

"We did. We danced, and I enjoyed it, despite myself. I felt sexy and daring. Then I realized he was likely Vivian's date, and I wanted him to be mine." Lana sighed and dreamily rested her chin on her hand. "He was a wonderful dancer, too. He didn't even step on me. We danced the second dance, and I realized I didn't even know his name."

"Who says you need to know his name if he's tall, dark, and handsome?" Jaime asked innocently.

Lana laughed. "Some of us have morals, Jaime. I think knowing something about a man is more important than how he looks. Here, it would have helped a lot. He's my new client. Well, he actually contracted me to work for him, not with him. What do you think I should do? I can't think straight when I'm around him."

"Oh, Lana, how are you going to handle not being in control of everything?" Jaime asked. "How is it going?"

"Honestly, I don't know," said Lana. "I'm furious with him right now, after he brought dinner to my apartment a little while ago, it clicked that he's wanting to buy the mill and my mom and dad's old place…"

"You had dinner with him? In your apartment?" Jaime interrupted. "Who are you and what have you done with my best friend?"

"It's not funny," said Lana. "He's got me moving into his office to work for a while, and I'm not even sure the arrogant jerk likes my ideas."

"I'm sure he liked something," said Jaime. "Just go with the flow, Lana. And think about his offer, but don't do anything until you're ready with your old house."

"I'm going to go by there tomorrow afternoon, make up my mind, y'know, but Garrett's driving."

"Don't worry," Jaime said, "just don't listen to that little voice in your head that tells you to run. And enjoy the kissing! Everything will probably work out better than you think."

"Thanks," Lana said dryly, "but I don't want to get involved with a client, and even if I did, there's the—"

"Don't you do it, Lana. We're the masters of our own destinies. There's no jinx. You've been around Kat too long. Geez. Look, here's my advice, don't work for him—get involved instead."

"Right—no!" Lana giggled. "Thanks J, not for the advice, but for always being here for me."

"Details, details." Jaime laughed too. "Be safe, cut loose, and get laid!"

Fifty minutes later, Lana hopped off her treadmill and fished a nightgown out of her top drawer. As she lay on the bed and closed her eyes, she allowed herself to think about Garrett's kisses one last time before vowing to put his sensuality out of her mind for good. Sexy fantasies crowded her thoughts as she lay there, happy ones she knew there was no room for in the workplace, but she couldn't bear the idea of banishing.

Garrett left Lana's apartment and drove toward the campground, slowing the car as he passed the old house place he planned to buy tomorrow. He glanced in the rearview and realized he was the only person anywhere. He parked the car right in the middle of the dirt road and got out of his rig. It was a world away.

The winter scene engulfed him. The silence was complete at first, then his hearing woke to the sounds of the country. Despite the cold, the river wove a song through the silence, a faint hum as it pushed icy water downstream, muffled by the crest of the hill the big house sat on.

The wildlife was all bedded down, likely trying to stay warm. He was the only creature stirring until an owl let out a mournful cry down by the old mill. Considering giving himself a mini tour, he decided he didn't need to be planning around it if he couldn't buy it. He needed it, though.

The house place was dark. He wouldn't go wandering around. It had to be Lana's decision, and if she wouldn't take his money, he would just have to build. But he would never make his deadline.

Well, at least not on the scope he planned. He could see it now. He would replace the wall on the riverfront side with glass walls and screened-in porches for a big open-air bar with a few reservable private dining areas for families or lovers. The kitchen was already in the house's front, so a basic remodel and he could at least have bar food and burgers by this spring.

In a perfect world.

He leaned on the hood of his rig, speculating again about

this property. He remembered the story. His grandparents had been very close with Lana's parents, and the tragedy had rocked the town. But that was a long time ago.

He scuffed around in the dirt a bit, then his eyes feasted on the vast sky. The stars fired his dreams. This was the amazing feeling he wanted to share, this sense of you, one-on-one with the universe. He felt it when he was a kid, then saw how the city lights and sounds blinded you from this feeling. He'd realized some people never experience the peace of letting nature completely fulfill them. That was when he'd begun working on this idea, to share it with as many people as he could. At least once in their life, let them stare into star filled skies and feel the magnitude.

He glanced at the old mill, thinking it would make a brilliant tourist magnet, then climbed in his vehicle, started it, and kicked the heat on high. It occurred to him he'd probably stood here an hour and not seen a trace of another human. Wild.

Driving past his grandparent's lodge home, he wished he could use his Pap as a sounding board, but it was late. Besides, they were moving into Riverbend Falls proper in just a month, with plans to travel. Garrett needed to count on himself. That meant working out his own problems.

In his new digs, he turned on the lights. He was making a mess of things already. Thinking of her, wishing she'd invited him back up to her apartment... They could have stayed in bed for days.

He thought things went okay, considering her obvious distrust of him. The way he was pushing her to do what he wanted her to do, he could hardly blame her. Despite the intelligence in his head reporting that he should back off and let her have her space, apparently his libido had made up its own mind. She appeared immune to his charm though, and unless they were kissing—generally wanted nothing to do with him.

He wished she were here to help him work off the nervous energy she generated in him. Throwing his blazer on a chair, he pushed his shoes off and slid out of his khakis, grabbing a pair of sweats out of the suitcase he had yet to finish unpacking. He wanted her in more than just his bed.

It hit hard because the truth was not helpful. He had it bad.

She was delightfully challenging to spar with, and he quickly developed grudging respect for the way she stood her ground. Tomorrow would be hard, because he needed to win, but he would make it up to her. He was looking forward to the challenge.

She was hot, smart, funny and… not interested. Why was he acting like a randy teenager? He had a lot to do if he was going to get the resort open by spring—he couldn't afford distraction.

Sitting on the weight bench that was just delivered with all his spanking new gym equipment, pride filled him. The deal they made him on his personal set when he bought a full gym package for the resort made it almost free, and he was going to have an appealing gym and spa set up in the lodge house. He pushed out several reps, the burn helping tamp down his annoyance. Only halfway thinking about how to steal another kiss tomorrow.

Chapter 6

Dread of this tomorrow had shadowed Lana for nearly ten years. It was dark and cold as she pushed through her morning workout, but the purpose she collected and the energy she generated pepped her up substantially. She decided she was ready to handle the day by the time she toweled off from her shower. She read e-mails and sorted through the week's mail. It was bills and junk, but also included a scrawled "thank you" letter from Hank Jenkins.

His wife, Mary, had passed away last summer. She had been the business end of his store, and he had no desire to learn the skills needed to keep it going. Lana had worked for several weeks getting everything in order for him to put the Hitchin' Post Farm and Feed on the market, so Hank could head up North and watch his grandkids grow.

Pinning the note on her bulletin board, she was especially pleased Hank was happy. She loved when someone appreciated her enough to thank her beyond the paycheck. Each client got her personal best and their happiness in note form was a special treat.

It was time. She had no choice. Tad needed her help.

At her desk, she re-stacked a few favorite paperbacks that had escaped the bookshelf and seized the harmless looking brown envelope. She shook the contents onto the shining gleam of cherry wood, grabbed her favorite pen from a cubby in the hutch, and settled in to do this.

There were a few stapled sheaths of paper, copies of her parents' Trust and Wills. On top lay a few white envelopes held together with a thick rubber band.

The documents read the way she knew they would. Tad had told her. The family's lawyer, Tom Peabody, had done everything her father requested. She was the one who hadn't pulled her own weight. It was an estate with no money, but precious land. The paperwork laid out the provisions for the property allocations. The homestead and Mill, and the twenty acres it sat on, were hers. Tad inherited the 500-acre tract of farmland and woods caught between the forest and the south bend of the river.

She pictured her favorite spot down below the house where powerful waves pushed over a long rock ledge, making one giant waterfall. The water never stopped in one place, worrying, it just kept joyfully splashing on, flowing freely. Like she should be.

Her dad made sure she could keep her happy place. He'd taught his children to fish there and was always teasing her about how back in the day, her mom taught mermaid school right under the ledge, and mermaids still lived there.

Her parents had been so wonderful. She missed them so much.

The first envelope was from Tom. It contained a formal release to close the Trust and release him from the obligations of the trustee, and an invoice with a separate ledger recording tax payments. She had a little money saved for her future, but according to Tom's note, he'd been paying property taxes while she avoided his requests to sign the paperwork releasing him. He'd kindly included a bill to current. The number made her wince. It would eat up every bit of her savings.

It was embarrassing, really, a detail girl who didn't pay her taxes.

Picking up her mermaid tail ink pen, she signed the paper, finalizing her parent's death after all these years. She avoided the emotional response, simply signed the release, then put down the pen and used a few calisthenics to redirect her mind.

The next envelope she recognized was what must be the cash offer for her inheritance. She chose not to open it. It was from Garrett, or rather, his attorney. If she hadn't been so moony-eyed at the dance the other night, she would have realized Garrett was buying Tad's land, and she wouldn't have been surprised when everything connected. She would have pieced the puzzle.

Today, she would decide without opening his offer so the cash wouldn't influence her. She'd loved her home on the riverbank. Selling seemed the last thing to do, but if she wasn't going to live there, what would she do with it? Tad wanted to sell a little land in order to make a better life for his boys. Why couldn't she consider selling to benefit her community?

Her eyes lit on the third envelope scrawled in her Dad's handwriting. She opened it with trembling fingers. Re-read it. The words hurt and healed. She didn't control the tears streaming down her cheeks as she read the soul searing words a final time.

Precious daughter,

If you are reading this letter, you've had to accept our last wishes too soon. This letter is a precaution against leaving unsaid a goodbye we pray you won't hear until we are very old. In the event something happened to both of us, we want you to do something for us, if you can.

Three generations of your Mom's family have gifted our home to the eldest daughter, and it's your mother's wish to continue the tradition. We hope you have many years of happiness surrounded by a loving family, as we did.

We pray the good Lord will bless you with a daughter of your own to keep the tradition alive. You're special, Lana, meant for great things. If your mother and I aren't there to be a part of the life you build, know we will always be with you in spirit. Be brave, my angel, and live your life to the fullest. We are proud of you and always will be.

Love Always ~ Dad and Mom

Lana sat back, the letter drifting to the shiny desktop. She had craved forgiveness for so long. Running from the emptiness of their home, but wishing for closure. Her always-practical father gave it to her from the grave. Why had she refused to accept this envelope from the lawyer? He'd called, mailed it to her several times. She'd refused his calls, mailed the paperwork back unopened.

If she refused it, she wouldn't have to accept what had become of her family.

He said they were proud, wanted something special for her, and she'd been running away. What was she running from? Memories of lost loved ones? Not logical. It took Tad to hand her the paperwork and ask for help before she would accept her responsibility. When had she become so self-absorbed?

She stood, stretched, thinking.

Garrett's ideas were... well, he would change everything, but he was going to, with or without her help. He'd already started. She wasn't sure she could stop him. His energy was infectious, though. Not sure what she wanted out of this deal, she was at least glad he was going with her to the old dwellings. She would see things with fresh eyes, through his eyes, and give it a chance.

She carefully tucked the signed paperwork in a return envelope, put a stamp on it, and tucked it inside her laptop bag beside her dad's note to carry with her. Her parents' wish for her couldn't come true this late in the game, but she could start acting like an adult, and do what was right. She was ready.

The black SUV was waiting when she stepped out. When Garrett saw her, he hopped out. Gracefully, despite the slick street, he came around and opened the passenger door for her. Clean shaven and dressed in some new looking jeans, he looked good. Raven black hair was wrestling around his collar in the brisk wind. He smelled very male. His dark blue eyes searched her face as she walked toward him, and he smiled, slow and sexy.

"Morning," he said as he motioned to a cozy looking leather seat.

Faint shadows under his eyes showed he hadn't slept well, and Lana secretly hoped he suffered as she had. On the upside, she hadn't had her nightmare. No, Garrett filled the few dreams she'd captured. She spent most of the night in that restless state between dreaming and wakefulness. His hands, breath, lips…

"Morning," she replied, climbing in. A heated seat. Wow! "I guess we're ready to do this?"

"That which does not kill us…" he quoted with a grin as he gently shut her door.

Tad came outside just as Garrett started around the vehicle. She hadn't told Tad where she was going today. She hadn't wanted questions.

"Well, here's a surprise. Garrett Wilcox! How are you, man? Have you talked her into selling then?"

"Tad, good to see you. I was just about to spirit her off and talk her into it, but we haven't gotten that far yet."

"Well, good luck." Tad cast a speculative look at her as she tried to ignore him. "I'd love to see the old place restored."

"Hello!" Lana powered down her window, wishing she hadn't heard the conversation. "Could you two quit?" Glaring at Garrett, she said, "I have not agreed to sell, and we were not about to discuss it. I agreed to give you a tour, just for kicks, later this afternoon. I haven't forgotten your needy itinerary. For me, this is about a job you hired me to do. I'd like to visit my new office first and foremost."

Then she spoke to her brother. "I told you I'd handle things with the lawyer. I wasn't lying." She waved the stamped envelope at him. "Dropping it in the mail today, although I'm sure he'll be out of the office until after Christmas. Garrett, c'mon. Let's get this over with."

"Okay, cool. Have a good day, sis," Tad called cheerily, and disappeared back upstairs. Obviously, he'd been checking on her. Men!

"Do you want to stop somewhere for breakfast?" Garrett asked, as he eased into the nonexistent traffic, passing straight through a snow devil that twirled in the street as they took off.

"I ate a cereal bar."

They drove the few minutes in uncomfortable silence until

Garrett slowed in front of her folks' abandoned place. From here, he could see the edge of the property he was buying from Tad, making the mill a friendly neighbor to the campground. He paused in the middle of the dirt road, where he had parked last night, looking at it, but Lana didn't even turn toward the structures.

"Later. We'll stop there on the way back."

Garrett chuckled. "So why don't you live there?" He pointed at the rambling three-story structure that eclipsed the riverbank, butting up to the woods with an overgrown garden spot on the far side of the clearing.

"What?" She glared at him.

"Fix up that old house and move in? We would be neighbors? I could be convinced to change my plans if you lived close. You could work for me full time."

"Fat chance. Can we stay on topic here? Right now, I'm more interested in seeing where I'll be working for the next three months."

"Sure, sure, on our way." Sitting so close to her, he wished he could keep his mouth shut. It was the light vanilla wafting from her soft skin, the honeysuckle smell drifting from her clean golden hair. He had no idea where his question came from. He already believed she'd sell and had plans drawn up for the contractor to modify the house as soon as he could push the deal through. The woman was pure distraction.

"Frankly, I'm still not convinced you need on-site help from an advertising specialist. Seems to me you need a secretary, perhaps a girlfriend," Lana added, her tone defiant.

"It's possible. But you're what I've got. Pap put a lot of hard work into building this business, and he built it with room to grow. He just didn't want to grow it. I do."

"Well, let's get on with it. I want to do my job and be done with this silliness because you drive me crazy. Where do you want to start?"

"Intriguing question," Garrett said, looking at her, noticing she still hadn't even glanced toward where she grew up. Her eyes were focused on the road, the bright green jewels shimmering with tears, a contrast against her pale skin. He didn't doubt she had every muscle in her tight little body contracted. "We started that on the dance floor."

"Hmph. I am about discovering what I'm supposed to do for your playground. I'm waiting for your guidance," she added, a little fierceness wiping away the sadness.

"Fair enough." She was right, of course; he was not here to seduce her, tempting as it was. He needed to keep his mind on his work. Longing. Her lips were a soft dream. She was the one, and he did not know how to go about getting her to accept it. At least getting her mad had given her some color.

"What did you do before you came here, anyway?"

She still didn't look at him as he eased down the road, but at least she was back to pretending polite conversation. He grinned. She might have relaxed a fraction when she cut her glance toward the river running parallel to the dirt road.

"Worked in restaurants. Line cook jobs, mostly, though I dabbled generously in house management. It was good money, but I always wanted to do it my own way and I've always wanted to come back here. When Pap and Gran said they wanted to retire and travel, I knew exactly what I had to do. I'm telling you, people in the city will pay out the nose just to sit outside and see a campfire. I never forgot the two weeks I spent here, and I can make it an even richer experience."

"Some people think this place is just fine."

"That's just it. It's not okay. The main street there in town looks like a belle ready for the ball with no suitor. I'll bring the life your town needs. I'll bring people. Revenues."

"So, your plan is an inclusive luxury guest ranch in the Ozark backwoods? Do you really think you can turn a campground into a year-round moneymaker with a few cabins? We are in the sticks."

"This is where nature is. And it may be a fantasy, but I think the fantasy will sell." Well, maybe not polite conversation, but they could work back up to that. He had poked her pretty hard. Right now, a huge hunk of his progress hinged on her agreeing to sell him her buildings.

Lana craned her neck to look through the windshield at the tall evergreens lining the road on both sides between her property and his. He could barely keep his eyes off her neck, wishing they could pull over and indulge in a few of his baser fantasies.

"Besides, that's where you come in, honey. We can start drafting the website immediately, and post a hiring page. Once we staff the place, we'll build a customer base that makes this out in the middle of nowhere place where everyone wants to be."

Rich laughter filled the cab, and he looked at her, surprised.

"Where are you going to find this staff? Not in Riverbend Falls." She shook her head. "Everyone gets out of here as soon as they're old enough. You'd need what, like thirty workers—seasonal workers—yet. That's like half the people who live here. They have jobs already, working farms and ranches... hardest in the summer. Believe me, those of us who stay here already have a life. We weren't just waiting for some resort to open so we could get jobs being housekeepers and canoe boys. You're dreaming, pal. I think you're about to use a lot of your own elbow grease."

He reached over and patted her leg as he turned down the long driveway flanked by an aging split-rail fence covered with snow in places. "We'll see. I'm not afraid of hard work." He grinned, a boy with a big toy as he looked out over his land, knowing his dream was shining in his eyes. "Forty employees by summer, I'd suspect. About half I'll keep full time. I plan to make this a year-round destination. Though granted, the float trips will be hotter in the summer. Let's see what we can pull off." He loved looking at her when she was all fired up. "Incentive is a useful tool. Here we are. Home sweet home."

Garrett realized he was home, a feeling he'd longed for as a kid.

"How did you get so much accomplished when you just got here?" she asked, a little wonder in her voice as she took in the cabins.

She stepped out of the rig next to the cedar lodge his

grandparents had called home for their whole married life. When he bought the campground, he assumed they would stay on, but Jasper insisted Emily wanted a small house, with traveling on her mind, so he'd upped the buying price and bought the lodge as well. They had used the money to buy a small house near the Post Office and seemed happy as pie about picking out a big RV after the holidays.

He would transform the Lodge into a clubhouse for guests, starting with the gym he just bought. Add to it as the dust settled. He imagined sitting on the screened-in porch watching over his guests as they enjoyed spending their money.

"Magic." He grinned. "Just kidding, I used the only real magic I have. Money. I hired a pretty decent contractor and his team to construct replicas of the original lodge and cabin Jasper designed. He's been working for months already, but he works offsite and ships the cabins to me and sets them in. I moved into the original cabin, built years ago, but the first three brand new mini lodges were just delivered yesterday. There are ten total. And that many smaller cabins that look like mine, which will probably better suit couples or fishermen, for delivery mid next month."

He pointed at miniature lodge cabins nestled between massive oaks. The oaks used to dot the campground randomly, but now they sheltered the cabins like they'd been grown around them.

"The post fence will be delivered next week, hopefully. I'm going to build a corral around each bunkhouse to create pockets of privacy, so guests get a feeling of exclusivity."

Her appreciation added to his own was a balm for his ego. Her enthusiasm would likely be a sexy driving force contributing to his success. A twist in his plan, since little of this was going the way he planned, but Garrett couldn't help imagining another twist or two he hoped they might try.

"Ready to look around?" He gestured she should lead the way, knowing he planned to check out her tight figure again. Wondering how to make her smile at him again.

Chapter 7

"Ready as I'll ever be," Lana said. *No, she was not.* Her warring emotions had her all stirred up, but she led the way. On one hand, she was glad to be a part of this, but it was all too close. Being at the beck and call of this infuriating, intriguing, impulsive man had Lana's nerves stretched so taut she felt tears lurking. She needed some breathing room…

"Want to go by the house first? I think Gran and Pap are…"

"No, let's get this done." Lana hated the grate in her voice. She sounded like an ogre, when really, she was barely holding it together. "I'd rather stick to the plan, I mean, and catch up with them later. The office?"

"All right," said Garrett. "You're all business, aren't you?"

"Definitely," said Lana, hoping it was true.

The office building triggered all kinds of memories. There had been some changes since she was a teenager, but her favorite parts remained—she could see why he wanted her to work here. The place had an atmosphere.

The interior boards were a rough aged oak. Made of the same material, standing sentry in the middle of the room was a long counter. Off to one side was an ice cream cooler, all dark and empty now. She could remember as girls being perched with Jaime and Kat on those aged cedar stools, trying to decide what flavor to choose.

The casual setup just soaked in and relaxed a person. She

glanced at Garrett and caught him watching her.

"I feel that every time. Like you walk in the door and you *know* you're on vacation." Garrett smiled and motioned her to walk around the counter. "I know it doesn't exactly look like it on paper, but I'm going to protect this in my own way. If this property would have gone on the market, they had a waiting offer from a farmer who wanted it to grow hay. I appreciate the need for places to grow hay, but not the business my grandparents spent their whole life building. I plan to build it up and share it. And make it my home."

"I can understand. It's beautiful." She would just have to convince him to accept a few more practical ideas. He was so deep and full of inspiration... she just had to process and not respond. As he showed her around, she watched his economy of motion, the cute way he pushed at his hair when he got excited. Lust butterflies were attacking her.

Did he have to look so sexy—so jumpable? She felt another blush creeping up her cheeks as she looked away.

"Are you okay?"

"I'm—yes, I'm fine." She walked down the hallway, encountering a wall of flat screen TVs and stacks of wall mounted tablets, a few desktop computers and software, all still in brand new boxes. "I'm just taking it all in. Did you rob an electronics store?"

"No, they robbed me. They delivered and unloaded, so we probably came out square. The office is through here." He gestured through an archway into a spartan room in the back, decorated mainly with surfaces holding paperwork. "I thought we could share it, but it will probably end up being more of a war room, anyway."

There were no chairs to speak of. It looked like a disaster site. Big ideas spread out everywhere. He had a ridiculously short time frame. It was just the two of them.

I am in way over my head.

"Can I have that?" She pointed at what looked like a big walk-in closet wedged across the hall, where several vacuums and mops had taken up residency. She leaned against the corner of his desk with feigned casualness. "For my space?"

He looked embarrassed for a brief second, then he was all confidence. "Well, sure, but actually, until you find me a friendly assistant manager, I was going to ask you to base out of the front office to help coordinate contractors and new staff." He grinned at her, unabashed.

She realized she should probably breathe again. She had a corner to call her own, a place to escape the overwhelming chaos that just seemed to whirl out of Garrett like a spin cycle on a washing machine. They had absolutely nothing in common. What was she doing here?

"I figure I'll be all over the grounds wherever I can be most effective pretty much every day until we open. And well, every day after that, too. I know this is more than a full-time job. But we can do it. Most of the employees will work outdoors or in other buildings. Now the bar is another hurdle. I want…"

Garrett was leaning his shoulder against the doorframe when his phone rang. He answered it and listened for a minute. He had it, just needed to find it. With a glance at her, and a shrug, she rolled her eyes at him, waving her hands over the papers to make it clear she could tell why he might not find something. That was worth a grin.

"I've got to find some information off the front desk for the building inspector," Garrett said, as he clicked off the call. "So many hoops to jump through. I can't wait to delegate some of this stuff to you. Do you want to wait or come with? It shouldn't take long."

"I'll wait here." Lana was glad for the space. She felt like a southern belle, nearly to swoon. A minute to herself would be good.

When he left, she assessed the mess. Bookshelves full of catalogs and campground management books stood against the wall, with more boxes of books stacked in front of them. A weathered peppercorn writing desk dominated the room despite being camouflaged by stacks of paperwork. There was, at least, an unopened package of manila folders laying on top.

She knelt, tracing the bold vines creating the legs of Garrett's desk. The man had good taste. Standing, she poked at a short stack of boxes containing printer paper, presumably his seat.

She rifled through the printed stacks, not disturbing anything, pleased to note some organization in the disorder. She found a stapled sheath of pages titled 'Bar and Grill.'

Lana looked toward the doorway where Garrett had disappeared. She wasn't snooping, exactly. The next page was an aerial view of her property. With no encouragement that she would sell, he had done massive amounts of planning, using her homestead for the site. The lead contractor was ready to go. She would have done that too, given the deadlines—but the nerve!

She flipped through the scrawled notes, noting a pencil sketch that detailed dismantling the house before restoring it with original fixtures and construction materials. It was a practical approach, but the home she remembered would be forever gone. Though that was the case already, as she'd abandoned the grand house to its fate when she ran away. Not sure she could live with that, she examined the rest of the figures and crude drawings outlining his highnesses intentions while it sank in.

The certainty that he had no genuine interest in her. He was doing what he had to do to get what he wanted for his business and she was like a love-struck pup, ready to roll over so she could get her belly scratched.

Another packet was entitled wedding plans, but it only contained generic notes on wedding themes. No details. Who was getting married? She stacked the paper back on the pile it came from and thumbed through the next stack. If there was anything else disturbing going on, she wanted to know now.

One stack of spreadsheets charted the company's growth since Jasper and Emily bought it nearly thirty years ago. She scanned the pages, noticing falling profit margins. The campground lost a lot of business in the last two years. The economy was rough, and it was true fewer people were vacationing away from home. She'd seen the results of that with several of her tourist-based clients.

Well, the lodging ideas Garrett was working on would bring

the profit margin back up. Some amenities would be pricey, though, and according to these figures, he'd given a lot more for the business than warranted based on the revenues. Since he was planning to keep the camping and canoe rental prices within the average family's budget, he'd planned to make his profits off lodging and liquor.

Another hand scribbled piece of notebook paper listed several ideas for drawing in business for different age groups. He planned a live music venue for the riverside bar area. Special offers for romantic weekends in the cabins—and she admitted the bed-and-breakfast packages would be a hit, if he could staff it. Family discounts with free inner tube rentals for the kids when you rent a canoe. He'd put a lot of thought into this.

Lana considered and her temper cooled. Smart plans. The lack of computerization would hurt, but she'd seen the new computers in the hallway and the expensive customer tracking software that was an industry standard. She couldn't fault his tactics—but the plans to destroy her house left her feeling off kilter.

Another page with the wedding plan title typed in bold print lay beneath, and she picked it up, hoping for more detail, then jumped like a cat when Garrett spoke from beside her. How had he come into the room without her noticing? She'd been so absorbed. She flipped the paper over—blank.

"I was going to apologize for taking so long, but I see as usual—you used your time wisely. Unfortunately, you rearranged my private papers. Not helpful. I know my system and I can barely find anything as it is."

Disapproval edged out his usual playfulness. He was treating her like a naughty child.

Lana had straightened as she browsed. Dadgummit.

He was making her nervous, a feeling she could use. Her cheeks flushed, but she pinned him with her own glare. Who did he think he was? When he was arrogant like this, she could handle him. It was the effortless charm he kept using on her that was keeping her off balance. She was proud her voice was confident.

"You just finished wishing you could start delegating to me, Mister-I-need-you-to-do-everything. This was not my idea." She waved the paper at him. "What are the wedding plans? Why are you hiding things from me? And this!" She reached over and shoved the stack with the house notes on top. "Our enterprise is not off to a peaceable start."

Garrett grimaced, obviously embarrassed, as he looked at the offending papers. "Sorry, I offered to pay you for the place, but my plans may seem forward since you haven't agreed. But... I haven't really done anything before of this magnitude, and I usually roll solo. It will take a little time for both of us, I think. I need you to work your magic, though. That's why I'm paying you so much. The wedding plans, well, those plans are a little further down the road. They won't affect you."

Lana bristled—he was so rude. But he was paying, and he was right. His personal life was none of her business. She'd focus on guarding herself against him. He was being such a player, flirting with her when he was to be married. She gestured to the stacked papers.

"You certainly are messy, Garrett. I straightened your desk but with this much disorganization, I'm sure you need a secretary. You could get a secretary cheaper. As a matter of fact..." she trailed off.

Garrett's eyebrow arched and that hungry look crawled over his blue eyes. The intensity startled her. She flinched when he abruptly leaned over, catching the back of her neck with a gentler hand. His mouth touched to hers, eliciting the response she was desperately fighting.

She leaned into him, returning the kiss, and he seemed to lose control for a minute. With a ragged breath, he pulled away to leave a short trail of sensual kisses from her mouth to her ear. "Like I said, babe, you're what I want," he murmured. Then he pulled back a bare inch, and with a mocking half bow and sweep of his arm, he motioned her to lead the way again.

Lana stared at him dumbly for a moment. Back to business as usual after what just happened? How could she gather herself... what was he, inhuman? How could he not feel the same distraction?

Lana tried to move, desperately, knowing she must not fall prey to his hypnotic kisses that nipped at every edge of her consciousness, but her legs felt cemented to the floor. Her will to get away evaporated. This was what she wanted. What a mess she was in now.

She mustered herself as much as possible, embracing sarcasm. "Aye, aye, cap'n. Your privacy is your own." She gave one last look at the stack of papers on the small desk and couldn't help herself. "Garrett, I wasn't intending to snoop, but I need to know. You said you didn't have a girlfriend. But I found the start of wedding plans?"

Garrett cut her off with a tight smile that did not reach all the way to his stormy eyes. "I don't. I'm used to going my own way, though, and sometimes I just roll with things rather than deciding exactly what it's going to be." With a deep sigh, he went on. "You're right. I asked for your help, and you're agreed to give me three months. I'll answer all your questions as we go on a brief tour and go over the plans."

The storm in him subsided as he talked, and he casually put his hand on her shoulder. She felt her breath hitch. Dadgum the man's impulsive gestures. There was no trace of resentment in his features and she wanted to turn into him, to touch his lips and see if they caught her fingers on fire, too. Details disappeared as her thought process slowed; she wanted. She didn't move, waiting for him to kiss her again. The heat felt so good, so right.

Garrett broke the spell, shifting his hand away from her shoulder, gesturing to the bright sunshine bouncing off the snow outside. He guided her toward it and pulled the door shut behind them.

"Yeah, okay." Lana was desperate to gather her dignity. Man. She was embarrassed. She told him not to kiss her. What was happening to her? "Let's go." Had she ever daydreamed like this before? Garrett was taking over her thoughts. Other kisses she'd experienced were a distant memory. It was past time to get a grip.

Besides, there was still the notion she'd been furious about ten minutes ago, that his attention was some kind of scam to get her property. Obviously, since he was planning a wedding. She would be strong, decide based on what she wanted, and deal with the emotional thing later.

"Well..." Yes, her voice was stronger this time. "Let's discuss your future."

A few minutes later, they stepped out of the campground office and her cell phone chirped. Seeing it was Tad, she angled around, looking for good reception. "Hey, what's up?"

"Sis?" His voice was shaky, upset. "I don't know how to say... There's been a fire. I was just leaving, and I noticed smoke under your downstairs neighbor's door. There was no answer when I knocked." His voice cracked. "Look, no one was hurt, and the fire department guys are getting the fire under control now, but... I don't think anything is salvageable."

"I'll be right there." Lana dropped the phone from her ear, and nearly dropped it in the snow. She closed her eyes, looking for strength. She couldn't find it. Her voice was far away, and she wasn't positive she spoke aloud. "There's a fire. I have to get home."

Lana's skin turned so pale Garrett was afraid she'd disappear. He swiftly got her to his rig and buckled her into the passenger seat, his mind racing. Her brother had disappeared back into the apartment. The fire... Now he saw black smoke billowing over the small metropolis of Riverbend Falls. "Lana, honey," he asked as he drove up the hill, "was that Tad on the phone? Is he okay?"

She opened her eyes but didn't lift her head from the headrest, as though the effort was just too much. "Yes. He's fine. Everyone's fine. The building, though. All my plants, my books—" She closed her eyes again, but her face remained blank of emotion.

"He's okay." Garrett thanked God and released the breath he hadn't realized he'd been holding. Lana was so fragile. He didn't think she could survive her brother dying in her apartment. "Let's see if there's anything we can do." He took her small icy hand in his for the five-minute drive back into town and he worried. The snow had melted from around the building and ash had blown everywhere, making the park across the street look like ash covered volcano drifts. There was a small crowd standing around the building, watching the fire brigade quench the dying embers.

Blackened and burned, the two-story building containing four small apartments was a total loss. The fire had started in the apartment under Lana's. Her place was a sub-floor with smoke drifting up from the carcass of her sofa. Garrett had liked that sofa, had imagined holding her on it.

Riverbend Falls' old pump truck and a newer truck from a neighboring town finally pulled away, and he wanted to put a healthy color back into her cheeks. She'd turned the color of the ash floating in the air.

"Look, you'll stay in a new cabin tonight and we'll think about tomorrow when it gets here." He noticed she gave him a strange look before he turned to Tad. "I have one you can stay in, too. I'm sure it would be good for her to have you close."

"Thanks man, I would, but I visited the old hunting cabin today up on the North hill and I'm going to build my house at the same site. I plan to poach a contractor from you any day now to help me put together a lodge kit I just ordered." He smiled to lessen the sting. "I just came by to let Lan know I was going to stay there tonight when… well, I'm glad I came. Heading out now, though. I'm exhausted."

He looked at Lana, who seemed unresponsive, and gave Garrett an assessing look before squeezing his sister in a tight hug. "Are you going to be all right, sis?"

Chapter 8

Lana roused herself from a daze, coming around to notice her brother talking to her.

"They say you're a hero. You even saved Ms. Goodwin's cat." She looked around at the dwindling crowd. "Where has everyone gone? Where will everyone live?"

"Ms. Goodwin and her cats are at the Inn and Out for now. Both tenants from downstairs are out of town. It looks like it was a faulty wire that caught fire on that back wall. Could have happened to anyone."

"It happened."

Her reedy voice worried Garrett. She looked near to breaking.

"Sounds like you can bunk at the resort tonight." He smiled wearily at Garrett. "So that's everyone."

At her confused look, Garrett spoke up. "Tad, come out to the lodge about noon tomorrow for Christmas dinner with our family. Gran insists you both come. I'm sorry this had to happen, but who knows what would have happened if you hadn't been here? Not all superheroes wear capes, man." When Garrett clasped Tad's hand, he felt a friendship forging. If he and Lana could just build on their foundation...

Why couldn't he just let her be? She sensibly wanted to keep their wits about them. Only… this of all times she should lean on him. A house fire was devastating. He could help if she'd let him take care of her, but she was as far away as she could be.

She had nixed pursuing what was stirring them both.

Having laid in a lonely bed the last two nights thinking about her—wishing—was maddening. He had to stop taking it so personally. She was not shy about not wanting to date him, and he needed to accept the cue. Only… the more he got to know her, the more he wanted to pursue his fascination with the girl he'd seen at the river so long ago.

More than professionally. He should let her out of this deal and give her some space, but he needed her. Someone he could count on to develop his vision, make it marketable. Lana was talented. She built a terrific campaign in one afternoon, just from his notes. Her ideas were modest, but he wanted to belong here, and she could teach him that, too. She suited him perfectly. Balance.

Right now, she was hurting, and he just had to make things easy on her.

"You can stay as long as you need and I'll do what I can if you need my help to find someplace to live. You'll have more privacy than you might in town."

"I need a lot of room…" Lana trailed off and he could tell she was thinking about the fire destroying her home, her things.

"It's a deluxe cabin with a luxury tub, a small gas fireplace and a formidable table for spreading out your notes while you think." Garrett avoided a rut in the road, avoided looking at her. "Pap is looking forward to your thoughts on the expansion. I told him you were helping me to take over in a not so hostile manner. Not sure he thinks that's possible, since I'm planning to more than triple the traffic down here. He's determined when he has his mind made up."

"So that's where you get it." She muttered under her breath. Hesitant, in a cool voice, she said, "I would be grateful for a place to stay through the holidays. The Inn will have several rooms open next week. If it's all the same, I'll handle it in a day or two. In the meantime, thank you. You've been very kind and

I feel a little dazed."

"You won't regret it." He glanced at her, noting her green eyes were glossy with tears, and hoped he was right.

She nodded, but didn't look sure.

"First things first. Let's find some food." He drove to the café around the corner.

She should walk away. No need to stick this torture out. There was nothing holding her now. If she had to start fresh... why spend any more time with this man who kept pressing in on all her safeties? She needed to think.

The table was in a corner, the checked tablecloths familiar to her. Kendra Rosati would mother her, just like before, when everyone felt sorry for her. How many times would her world go up in flames?

She toyed with the ketchup bottle, avoiding that line of thinking. Some living just had to be done. She didn't take many risks, but that was a freak accident, not something any amount of self-protection could have avoided. Except for her plants, it was just things. Her favorite book collections, authors who amply filled long hours... Things she'd loved, but nothing irreplaceable.

The restaurant was empty and the tabletop intimacy was stifling. The only sounds coming from the kitchen were occasional pots bumping and a radio quietly repeating the forecast. The snow would melt away in a day or two if the weatherman was right.

These were the motions she needed to go through. Just keep functioning. She watched Garrett as he surveyed the menu, a slight wrinkle in his brow making his eyebrows wiggle occasionally. His sensual mouth was moving as he read the menu items aloud. She indulged in the rousing memory of his lips against hers. The thought might banish the hazy depression trying to settle over her.

When Kendra came by the table to take their order, she slid in briefly and grabbed Lana in a big, sympathetic hug before sliding back out of the booth to her spot. "Do you want your usual, honey?"

Lana shook her head, feeling no desire for food. "Just coffee with cream."

"You're usual," Kendra nodded with determination, and made a note on her pad without looking at it, smiling at Garrett.

"Ah, I'll have a bowl of minestrone, and some of that amazing smelling bread. I'll take a cannoli, too, just for good measure. Tall water... coffee too, black."

Kendra gave Lana a surprised grin and a wink. "Two usuals, coming up."

Garrett tried to distract her. He told stories about working in different restaurants and in different towns, but Lana barely heard. She'd started doing leg flexes under the table.

Despite his efforts to shoulder them, her troubles were her own, and she would cope. She always did. However, the intriguing complexities of the guy across from her who ordered her favorite meal were hijacking her rational self. She could just walk away.

When Kendra placed the bowls and dessert plates down, Garrett did not miss the coincidence, either. He poked at her across the table, trying to provoke a grin. "You have good taste, or I do. It seems we have more in common than you thought, Lana."

She didn't respond, just began spooning up Kendra's life affirming minestrone. It was heaven. They ate, Garrett talking and eating enough for the both of them as she picked at hers, thinking.

She needed to work out a new plan—could she have a clearer sign it was time to move on? Nothing held her here except... everything. Now Tad was home. Could she really leave now when her brother might need her? The boys would be down in the summer, and he would surely need some babysitting. She'd barely met the youngsters, and they were her only kin.

The real problem... was she afraid to leave and afraid to stay? Afraid to commit to a *different* path. What if the big world was just as lonely as Riverbend Falls? But could she stay here, work for Garrett, and stay sane?

She could, but she shouldn't. Should she? This was her territory. She couldn't let him run wild. If the old timers, aka the town council, turned against him, they would shut him down faster than nobody willing to work. Which would also be a problem. She grimaced, dreading the meeting she was sure would be in her near future.

If she could just convince him to give her space, she could check into the Inn, or stay at Kat's place. She was out of town, but she wouldn't care. She just needed to get her bearings...

"I can hear the wheels turning in your pretty head, Lana," Garrett said. "I don't think you can shake me just yet. Even if it's far from ideal, it's a challenge, isn't it? But I think we should get going. I'm taking you to see Gran." He stood and dropped a few bills on the table. Threw an extra one on top and hollered toward the empty sounding kitchen, "Merry Christmas!" No one else had even come into the restaurant.

Lana shrugged into her coat, noting sadly to herself that what she had on was what she owned. In the rig on the way to the resort, she dozed.

Lana stared out the open window. The sun was bright, and there was a brisk feeling in the wind. The temperature was comfortable. She looked around the old station wagon, surprised to see her hand resting on Garrett's blue jean wrapped thigh. It regrettably thrilled her to see him, but something felt off. The wind was blowing his raven black hair all askew and his powerful jaw sported a sexy stubble, creating a feeling of wild anticipation in her.

She smiled, tried to ask where they were going. No words. Oh no! She touched her throat, willing it not to be. No sound, nothing. Her question morphed into a soundless whimper. She looked at Garrett, hoping for reassurance, and there was none. Her dad was driving and day had darkened to night—the headlights hurt her eyes. Lana knew this dream. She tried to scream. She was terrified of what would happen when the car left the highway and reached the place where the old oak timelessly waited.

Lana tried to close her eyes. How could Garrett have done this to her? They reached the tree and Garrett's voice replaced the slow sounds of metal crushing and glass breaking. "I won't let anything hurt you."

Lana sat up abruptly in the seat, shaking. Her dream Garrett woke her before the plunge. She glanced sideways at his profile as he drove her down a bumpy dirt road and pulled her arms to her chest. What was going on? Why was he pushing his way into her organized life, stealing her heart? She felt worse when she realized she was glad he was there.

The pain that tortured her consciousness every night had failed today, on Christmas Eve, when real life had given her both a chance to heal from the pain and fresh pain to adjust to.

"Garrett, I don't want to do this. I want to check into the Inn. I'll talk to your grandparents for you, but then I want to leave." Her feelings for this self-assured creature who was the most stimulating man she'd ever met and had to work with— no, for, tormented her.

She couldn't avoid him, and wondered if she wanted to. Didn't matter, though. Her integrity counted. She'd maintain boundaries and get the job done. Then she'd forget all about Garrett Wilcox, take her money, and decide what to do then. Later. Maybe she'd buy a big house without neighbors to burn it down, and start again. She needed to do something risky. She could get a dog... she would get a puppy.

Sure, she could adjust. Three months of servitude. Then she'd have enough to start up in New York, or somewhere like Paris—a long way from impulsive men who disrupted plans.

Clicking her tongue impatiently, she wondered why she had to convince herself. Nothing changed for her just because Mr. High and Mighty requested her services as an assistant. Because that stung her ego.

As they passed the old grist mill building, heading to the Wilcox land, Lana thought he meant to ignore her, then he spoke. "Look, Gran would be heartbroken to know you'd rather stay elsewhere when she's already prepped a cabin for you."

"Mr. Wilcox, how long do you intend to keep manipulating me to get your way?"

"Manipulating you? I don't think..."

"Never mind. I wouldn't think of hurting Emily's feelings, but don't think we can work together and I'm going to allow you to continue manipulating me. I will not fool around with a man who is promised to another."

"Not manipulating, Lana—wait, what? I'm not promised to another. I just thought if you could come here and..."

"I said I would help you talk to them, but I prefer my space, and I'm here purely for business reasons. If you agree to maintain the same standards, I am at your service. Professionally speaking. How long do you intend to keep me out here, Mr. Wilcox? I'll need to find another place to live..."

"Lana, are we back to formalities? Don't pull away from me. I know you're hurting."

Lana sniffed. "I'll call you Garrett if you insist, but sir, our relationship is formal, a business relationship, and I shall endeavor to keep it so. How long?"

Lana's gracious nature was taking over despite her desire to remain contrary. She admitted to herself a cabin here at the river would be far less stressful than a room in town where sympathies would pour over her... "Poor Lana, she's lost everything again..."

Hopefully, she could maintain a cool distance and get her act together quickly. That would help. If he hadn't been so high-handed, deciding things for her, she probably wouldn't have lost her temper.

She was off kilter, though, and had gotten ticked off again. Now she would have to work hard to be professional instead of seeming cross. She didn't like it. He was getting the wrong impression of her. He muddled her ability to communicate.

"I accept your hospitality, and I appreciate the accommodations you've prepared," Lana said, then caught herself. Try not to be so stiff.

"I'll have to borrow some clothes, perhaps from Emily,

because if I remember correctly," she paused, teasing him, finger on her lip thoughtfully, "you have little besides Armani. I'll need to go shopping, too, I guess. Everything will be closed for Christmas tomorrow, though."

"We'll rough it, camping style," Garrett said.

The decision-making helped, and she brandished confidence she didn't feel. "I'll work tomorrow before lunch at the campground, since we have your notes. You don't mind working on a holiday? We'll need every minute we can commit." She patted her bag, wishing she'd put a lot more in it before she left her place. She'd brought her work in case she'd needed to make notes, but couldn't she have tucked in the Viking novel she'd nearly finished? But she also had the letter from her dad. There was strength in that. Another step.

She would throw herself into this job, worry about her losses... later.

"Lana, honey, bless your sweet heart. You look worn to the bone. So sorry about the fire, what a sorrowful mess..." Lana started to respond, but Emily Wilcox pulled her in the door without pausing for a breath. "Sweetheart, you come with me. I know just what you need." Emily linked her arm with Lana's, then paused, turning back. "Garrett, dinner will be at seven, so if you have something else to do this afternoon..." Emily sent her grandson a look.

He didn't protest as she effectively dismissed him.

Emily patted her stylish, smooth, white hair and took a deep breath. "Lana and I must get re-acquainted. I have some tea for us in the den, then she'll be resting until dinner. I'll see to it."

"Yes, Gran. It seems I've thought of something to do after all. I'll see you ladies at seven." Garrett smiled charmingly at them and disappeared, finally.

"Lana, sweetie, let's get some hot tea in you. You're pale as a ghost. Don't worry about a thing. These are terrible circumstances, but Garrett is a good boy. Full of big plans. Maybe it's fate that brings you down to the river this Christmas. It'll be mine and Jasper's last one here at the lodge. We bought the little farmhouse out near the post office. I've always thought it looked so peaceful. No campers running around at all hours of the night. Garrett tells me you're going to work your magic on his campground—excuse me—resort expansion." She grinned. "Are you looking forward to it? I suppose I'm glad to see this place grow. I'm just glad there's someone younger to do it. These old bones..." Emily stopped briefly, motioning for Lana to drink more tea. "I get carried away talking, so nudge me if you want to answer."

"Please, you've been so kind already." She was just relieved to think clearly, and grateful for Emily's ability to calm her. She was a small woman, but her big personality was warm and comforting. The atmosphere in the den was settling too, with its large wooden beams and American Indian motif. A four-foot tall resin of a brown bear cub looked up at her realistically from its perch on a stump, offering her peppermints from a candy dish.

"Lana, I doubt my grandson noticed, but you're perilously close to tears, honey, and I suspect he's responsible for a part of that turmoil."

Lana nodded miserably, embarrassed at being so transparent. Emily gathered her into a brief hug and sat back to listen.

Garrett stopped by the new cabin Lana would stay in, but Emily had taken care of prepping it before they arrived. He looked around with an eye for detail, proud of the contractor's work. He'd hired the man based on Jasper's recommendation, and this cabin was nice and tight, built to replicate the lodge, but with more personalized amenities in the smaller space.

His friends from the city would expect every convenience if they deigned to trek out here to the wilderness. With Lana's help, Garrett would be prepared to knock their socks off this summer and relieve them of a lot of the money they teased him he wouldn't make out here in the boonies.

He'd hoped to spend the rest of the day with Lana picking her brain, but Gran had her own ideas, it seemed. Lana was thawing toward him, despite being upset, and he hoped for a full thaw. If she'd just lean on him a little, he could do so much to smooth her path. She was so blasted independent.

Since he'd picked her up that morning, her mood changed several times—back and forth between frosty cool professionalism and excitement about her surroundings. Then she'd gotten that awful call and handled it like a rockstar. He couldn't resist the intricacies of her weaknesses and strengths.

He needed to work off some of the tension building in him since he first kissed her. She'd had such a powerful effect on him in such a short time. He crossed the grounds and disappeared through the shrubbery to his cabin, which wasn't visible from the lodge. Here, he could be himself.

He was finding life so different here. Having attended military academies and an Ivy League college, he'd learned that, especially in the workplace, most people respond immediately to the orders of a man who is confident in his decisions. Here, this laid-back community was making him feel very conspicuous, and he hadn't even gone public with his plans yet. He needed to learn to fit in somehow. Right now, though, it was just him, and he could chill.

Garrett decided a little soul food would go a long way. He reached into one of his food stashes and pulled out a bag of potato chips. He ate several handfuls, then carefully tucked them away. His obsession with junk food had always been discouraged, and he thought about Lana's cereal bar breakfast. It sure contrasted with her ability to put away a burger with the works and two orders of fries.

His kind of woman. Garrett smiled to himself as he grabbed a soda from behind the orange juice in his fridge. He kept secret stashes of junk food everywhere, since he'd been a kid. Now he kept it out of sight for habit's sake, but it was funny, he thought, a grown man who hid the fact he ate potato chips.

Garrett wandered into his bedroom, a room packed full of gym equipment, turned on his stereo, and cranked up the volume. He picked up his weights and lost himself in oblivion for a while.

He thought of the beautiful woman in his grandmother's

care, the woman who seemed to cure him of the lonely ache he'd borne since childhood. That was when he realized his parents weren't just busy, they didn't want him. He wondered if there was any hope of making her want him, or if his path was meant to be traveled solo.

Chapter 9

Lana enjoyed seeing Emily order Garrett around after the way he'd maneuvered her. Clearly, he was used to getting what he wanted. The respect he'd showed his grandmother enchanted her, though. Respect for elders was drilled into Lana, a trait sometimes lost on outsiders. Before seeing how he'd responded to Emily, she would've bet Garrett argued every point. It was a surprise to learn he possessed any genuine sensitivity.

She'd wept her story onto Emily's shoulder and told her about the nightmares that cropped up this time of year. The story of her last ride home with her Mom and Dad. Emily had hugged and patted her while she cried, leaving Lana calmer but exhausted beyond belief. She hadn't realized how much she was still beating herself up for her mistakes. It was in the past. She was fine and everything was under control, wasn't it?

Emily dried Lana's tears and walked her to her cabin, pointing out interesting plants and flowers, mostly dormant and snow covered now, but the ground-hugging holly and ivy and the tall pine and spruce trees made everything pretty and Christmassy. She also told funny stories about camper mishaps and tall tales about fish and deer. At the cabin, Emily looked sad for a moment, then smiled in a way that lit up her friendly eyes.

"Whatever will be, will be," she said. "Garrett loved this place when he was young. I always hoped he would choose to land here. There's another cabin, one Jasper built when he built the lodge, that's been here forever over there..." She pointed toward a tall hedge, and Lana noticed a small opening that kept the woods separated from the yard. Emily continued... "he calls it his man cave. Now that we're retiring, I'm looking forward to leaving all this headache behind and having Jasper all to myself. I have a long honey-do list." She giggled like a teenager at a slumber party. "Anyway, I hope you find everything comfortable. If you need anything, just ring the house and we'll see what we can do. I laid you out a few changes of clothes and a nightgown and robe. Can you think of anything else, sweetie?"

Lana took Emily's hands in hers to show her appreciation for the older woman's kindness. "Everything is already far better than I could have hoped for. Your home is enchanting and I'm sure I'll be very comfortable. Thank you for letting me cry on your shoulder," Lana added shyly. "That's not... usual for me."

Emily smiled kindly. "Anytime, honey, anytime. I'll send Garrett to escort you to dinner when it's time. I know Jasper is eager to visit with you."

Lana hesitated. "Sure, that would be fine. Thanks again for having me."

As Emily walked across the yard back toward the main house, Lana looked around at the earthy décor and high beams in the log cabin, then bounced on to one of the most comfortable beds she'd ever been on. She closed her eyes, putting out of her mind the image of her own lovely bed smoldering.

Jasper entertained Lana at dinner with delightful humor and a sharp mind, despite his age. It provided another clue about some of Garrett's more likeable personality traits. She'd always liked Jasper, but his business sense surprised her. He'd seemed an absent-minded grandfatherly type with little on his mind beyond the weather as he cheerfully gave away candy from his pocket and visited with anyone who stopped to talk.

He was interested in the ideas Lana and Garrett were debating about prices, campground amenities, boat rental rules, and the like. He challenged nearly every new idea, and either conceded or argued, but there was no middle ground. The conversation was vibrant and full of spunk, and despite his silver white hair, Lana could tell he resisted a quiet life.

"This is not a rich neighborhood, my boy. You'll out-price yourself if you get hoity-toity." Jasper was almost pleading for someone to argue with him.

"I agree, Jasper." Lana gave Garrett an 'I-told-you-so,' look. "Most of the folks around here already run a tight budget."

"That's right." Jasper was nodding approvingly in Lana's direction. Emily was grinning, seeming to enjoy the banter as much as the tender pork roast. "Garrett, I'm glad you hooked up with this little lady. She is bound to bring common sense to whatever schemes you're cooking up. I can't think of a better gal for the plans you mentioned for next year. What was it again? Some romantic angle?"

Lana noticed Garrett was uncomfortable when he glanced at her. She'd accidentally been staring at him again, so she didn't miss that he had a secret. "A large part of my plan is catering to some new business, yes."

"Well, if you'll just scrap those ideas of yours about selling fancy dinners and having hoity-toity wine tastings, and stick to selling hamburgers and ice cream, you'd do better," Jasper said with a hint of frustration in his voice. "If I've said it once, I've said it a hundred times. Keep it simple."

"I know, Pap. Like I always say, I can do it all. Once I bring tourist money to the town, the locals have less tight budgets, their kids stay and get jobs, we all win. I consider it simple."

"But if you'll just back off and work on the locals, we don't need a bunch of tourists around here..." Jasper said.

Emily interrupted. "Jasper, for heaven's sake. You've been running a tourist-based business for nearly thirty years. You cater to locals because they're your fishing buddies..."

Garrett grinned. "Thanks Gran. Don't worry, Pap, I'll take good care of you and your fishing buddies. I've decided about the resort. It's good business. It'll work, with Lana's help."

Emily smiled lovingly at her husband. "Jasper's determined, Lana, and once he gets started, you get to hear all his ideas until he can convince you they were yours." Everyone laughed, but Lana was secretly pleased to find an ally in Jasper. She noticed a striking resemblance between his ideas and the original ideas she proposed.

Garrett wasn't paying much attention to the table conversation. He was watching her. Staring even, the way his grandparents were ogling each other. Warmth traveled from her neck to her toes. Finally, Emily suggested they move into the kitchen for dessert and coffee. Lana could barely concentrate. She wanted to get lost in the stormy blue eyes focused on her. She ached to experience the tenderness Emily and Jasper seemed to share.

Oh, to throw caution to the wind, and admit she was enjoying herself... but she couldn't forget she was cursed, destined to doom any relationship. Even if she could get past the jinx, he was hiding something. If that something was another woman and he was just hoping for a last fling before he got married, well, she was a grown woman. As long as she knew the stakes, she'd... deal with it tomorrow. Enjoy herself now.

The food, the atmosphere, the company... everything came together to give her a sense of belonging, something she'd missed since her parents died. Like that young girl, she was afraid the feeling couldn't last.

After dessert, Emily insisted Lana be allowed to rest up for Christmas festivities the next day. She gave Lana a motherly hug and whispered, "I'm so glad Garrett brought you. I knew he wouldn't settle for less than the best."

Embarrassed and touched by the notion she'd been approved left Lana's thoughts jumbled. "Good night, you two. Thanks again for your hospitality."

"Let me walk you to your cabin, Lana. I'm headed out, too." Garrett hugged Emily and gave Jasper a hearty clap on the shoulder.

"It's been a genuine pleasure, Lana." Jasper said with a wink. "You kids be good, so Santa will come."

Garrett held Lana's jacket for her and pulled his own on before opening the back door for her. They stepped out into the crisp air and trudged through the snow toward her cabin.

"Are you having a good time?" Garrett asked.

"Under the circumstances, wonderful. Everything is beautiful here, it'll make a fine resort. I'm sorry I'm not sleeping in my own bed, but it's nice of you to take me in."

"There are more things I can't wait to show you. Thanks for coming. My Pap is something else, isn't he?"

Lana laughed. "I can see a remarkable resemblance, Garrett. After talking to both of you, I can see why you were desperate for outside counsel."

"Yes, counsel…" he muttered. Clearing his throat, he slowed down and reached for her arm. "Tomorrow, let's be friends, not co-workers, or whatever has you irritated with me? I'm looking forward to the holiday stuff tomorrow, okay?"

They stood, not moving, despite the cold, and Lana shivered. "I… Yes, I'd like that. But just friends—there isn't going to be anything more between us, OK?"

He didn't respond, and Lana didn't know why she agreed to concede any ground at all with him. He wasn't part of her plan. It felt right and wrong, confusing at the very least. Moving toward her cabin again, Garrett's step was lighter, and he smiled at her, his firm jaw showing a shadow of stubble in the moonlight. When they arrived at her door, he reached for her hand and kissed it softly. The air intensified between them, filled with unspoken longing.

"I bid you adieu until the morn, river goddess," Garrett teased, lightening the intensity. He turned and walked away and Lana watched him wistfully from the steps before she stepped inside and went to bed.

A few hours later, she was bathed in sweat, jolted out of sleep by her nightmare. She desperately tried to remember where she was. The cabin. The nightmare left a bitter metallic taste in her mouth, and she got out of bed in search of water.

She wandered around a bit after quenching her thirst and did several stretches and yoga poses as she thought about Garrett. A short time later, feeling better, she went back to bed, smiling ridiculously. Garrett was so sweet when he walked her to her cabin last night. Her eyes fluttered open and dread set in—she realized she was falling for him! That was not good. She closed her eyes again and slept untroubled for the rest of the night.

Warm morning sunlight streamed through the windows and Lana flexed her ankles luxuriously in the soft bed. It was Christmas day, and she felt good despite the familiar sadness of loss. She got up, stretching her body long and straight, thankful she was still early. Time for twenty minutes of yoga and a shower.

When she soaped herself under the hot spray, she thought of Garrett's situation. He was so determined to go his own way, despite Jasper's encouragement to cater to the locals. She could understand. He was investing a lot in this and without a full body count during the summer months to fill his boats and lodging, the off-season wouldn't balance.

Jasper should understand that too, since he had surely felt their shrinking profit margin. So many of the old timers resist change, though. Lana grinned at herself. Okay, even young people might resist change, because change presents complications. She wondered about Garrett's long-term plans, the ones he hadn't shared with her. It was strange the way he reacted when Jasper mentioned a new angle, and Lana wondered what the deal was. She vowed to herself to find out. If it was another woman, despite what she wanted, she would walk away from this whole deal. Man, she'd never been so wishy-washy!

Garrett himself? The man was a walking contradiction. Maybe she could learn more about what he was up to today while watching him interact with his family. If not, she would ask him directly again when they started working on his campaign.

Her stomach gave a nervous flutter at the thought of working so closely with him, and she sat on her bed, afraid again. She couldn't be falling for him. Or if she was—he could never know. The side effects of knowing Garrett were not as bad as the arrogance of the man himself, so what he didn't know couldn't hurt her.

She would enjoy herself on this job. How could she not? She was to have a part in changing Riverbend Falls forever, hopefully for the better, then... then she would move on. Definitely with a dog. As she stepped out of the shower, she heard a knock on the door. She wrapped a towel around her head and pulled on the robe. She answered, hoping Emily sent breakfast so she would have a reprieve from Mr. Wonderful this morning. No such luck. Garrett carried a breakfast tray, and on the tray lay a yellow rose.

"Merry Christmas! Did you sleep well?" He watched her nod slowly before he asked, "I know it's too early for you to be ready, but want some apple pancakes? Have breakfast with me?"

Lana smiled, flattered despite herself. "Sounds yummy. I love apples, but that's far more food than I usually eat in the morning." As she stepped back to let him in, she realized with horror she was still wearing only a bathrobe and a towel. "Oh..." she said, panicking.

Garrett took charge. "Well, I know my way around in here, so if you want to finish dressing, I'll set us up in the dining area." He wiggled his thick, black brows playfully a few times. "Not that I don't like what you're wearing..."

Turning red, a touch of irritation gave Lana the edge she was hoping for. "Focus on the food, will ya! Geez, men!" She stalked off toward the bedroom, smiling.

Garrett watched Lana hurry back into the bedroom, aroused again by the sway of her tight frame. Something about her made him crazy to get closer. They'd only known each other a few days, but he felt like he'd been waiting for this woman a long time. He would find out what was holding her back and fix whatever was bothering her so he could handle the sensual woman underneath her prickly exterior.

He had talked with his Gran this morning, and she warned him against pushing Lana too fast. He explained he wasn't pushing, just not backing down. Emily had given him a look that said she didn't believe him.

"Be friends with the girl first, Garrett. If it is meant to be, everything will fall into place," she'd advised. Like a woman to think friendship was the answer.

Sure, he wanted to be friends, but he ached to be closer. Patience was not one of his strengths. He would teach her how to have a good time, sweep her off her feet. He could draw her out of her shell. She was hot and talented… and emotionally unavailable. Surely, she wished for romance. He'd seen the lusty romances stacked around her apartment.

After hashing out ideas that night, he'd wondered why he was so determined. She ran hot and cold with him, mostly cold. Judging by her shiny work ethic, she wasn't likely to be the kind of girl who would play around for fun. If he could get her into bed, would it be enough? She got under his skin in a sexy way, but she was too serious for someone who intended to have fun for the rest of his life.

He didn't want to go back to being the serious Garrett. Thankfully, he hadn't married the girl he'd been engaged to in France. It had seemed storybook perfect at first, him an American studying under a renowned French chef. His beautiful daughter wanted so badly to come to America, and she'd convinced him she'd fallen in love with him.

His mother had approved of Felice, possibly the first thing Garrett had ever done she approved of, and the two women set to planning a wedding. With the respect due a woman who saved her virginity for her wedding night, Garrett left her mostly alone to make plans while using his resources to ensure her happiness.

Several things began bothering him about Felice. He was feeling useless, an extra actor in his own wedding. There were other things... It wasn't that he wasn't in love. He had never believed love to be the driving force in a marriage, anyway. It was that she was bent on molding him into a lifelong suit and tie, and after his years in a rigid boarding school, he'd already determined that wasn't the life for him. He told her so, but it had little impact on her plans for them. He preferred to relax a little in his adult years.

One day, just weeks before the wedding, he stopped by the restaurant on his day off to put in a food order he hadn't had time to put in the day before. He discovered Felice and the prep cook going at it in the supply closet. It was clear she was no longer a virgin. Garrett packed up and came home, refusing her excuses. He didn't intend to open himself up for that type of manipulation or betrayal ever again. Perhaps he even better understood his own father's emotional unavailability.

It didn't matter now, though. He was here and doing things his way. His Pap tried to pretend it wasn't important to keep the company in the family, but Garrett understood he was trying to shield Garrett from the responsibility of being the last heir to the land. He was 30 years old now, and it was high time for him to be building a family... He made a mental note to make some contacts regarding adoption once he got the resort running smoothly. His grandparents supported him in the notion, and his parents lost their right to an opinion long ago.

Lana walked back into the room, still glowing from her shower and wearing bellbottom jeans and a green silk patterned blouse that flared at the wrists. Garrett stifled an urge to gather her close, seduce her mouth, and devour her an inch at a time until she begged for more. Instead, he bowed gallantly. "Breakfast awaits the blue jean queen."

She looked down at the outfit, blushing. The jeans wrapped around her rear very tightly, and her smallish boobs, in this sixties style blouse Emily had obviously dug out of an attic, looked plump and swollen, creating an insane amount of cleavage.

"I think Miss Emily had to dig pretty deep for clothes in my size. I lucked out for dinner last night but, flower child it is for today, I guess." She smiled sheepishly and looked over at the spread he'd arranged on the little bistro table, the rose in a vase he'd found in the kitchenette. "Why are you being so stinkin' sweet?"

"Am I?" Good. "You look beautiful. Now eat up. We don't want our pancakes getting cold."

After breakfast, they spent several hours in what would serve as Lana's new office. They rearranged furniture, looked through catalogs, and tracked down likely suppliers for getting basic needs for the campground general store. They brainstormed on what to stock in the gift shop. Garrett wanted to mimic an old country store, so they discussed involving a few locals who made their own jellies and jams and might be willing to market them through him in order to add validity to his enterprise. He planned to have a bakery that would sell fresh baked sweetbreads, and resurrect the ice cream bins so he could sell hand dipped cones in the store.

Next, they set up computer stations. One in his office, her office, one at the entrance, and another two computer stations behind the front desk. Finished, Garrett turned to find Lana staring at him, a very confused look on her face. She was about to give him the boot. He could feel it.

Keep her close, his brain commanded. He moved in and took her face in his hand, gently drawing her to him until their lips touched and passion exploded. She pressed her body into his like a second skin, and he felt nothing but overwhelming desire.

His feelings intensified as she deepened the kiss, her arms lacing around his neck, and it almost felt like they were one. His tongue explored her mouth, pushing passion to the breaking point. The words she planned to say earlier morphed into a lusty moan that jerked her up straight. The loss of her closeness crushed him as she stepped back to gather herself.

"Wow," Garrett breathed. "That's some pair of lips."

Lana flushed, angry. "This simply isn't working. We aren't working."

Chapter 10

"Working pretty well for me, babe." He looked around the office. "We've accomplished a lot today. Yep, you're just the girl I need." An amused expression on his face made her furious.

"No. I can't work with you. This isn't how I do business. I'll get you someone else…"

"No, yourself." Garrett rested his hands on the shoulder high counter behind her, wrapping her in his arms without touching her… Again, she found his lips inches from hers. "I hired you because you're the best. I want you and no one else will do."

Dread skittered through Lana as she watched his excitement grow and she envisioned herself alone, pining for him. When she completed this contract, she would leave town, or worse yet, stay here, living a dull life while he went on his exciting way. Their lifestyles were simply too different to mesh well. They had different goals, dreams that didn't include each other. There was no way she could tolerate his impulsive lifestyle, it just couldn't work.

She needed to distance herself from him physically— emotionally. That was the real problem. It was time to ask

Garrett about his wedding plans. That had to be cleared up first because it would be hard to handle if she found him promised to another.

She ducked under his arm and walked around the desk, waving at the ideas they'd been roughing out. "As an assistant, right? Or what? I've been making competent decisions for my clients for a long time. I wonder at your real motives. You can't convince me to sell you my land any better from your bed than from an office. You don't have to trick me." Her freaking lip quivered.

"You sure seem to assume a lot." Garrett's rough voice was dangerously quiet. "Maybe you should ask me about whatever's on your mind, instead of talking out of your head, trying to distract yourself from the fiery feeling in your belly."

Lana gasped. "How dare you, you pig!"

"Deny it," Garrett said. "Deny you want me, as bad as you know I want you."

"You are conceited, Garrett Wilcox, and no woman in her right mind would intentionally get tangled up with you." Would be nice if she could access her right mind when he was around. "If you won't accept a replacement, Garrett, we have to lay some ground rules."

"Some rules, huh?" Garrett's voice softened as he came around the desk to embrace her again.

She pushed his hand away. "For instance, no touching. At least, no—no touching. It messes up my concentration. Don't mistake my staying for anything but professionalism. I can't wait to finish this job and go back to my life." Even if it might be hollow again. Garrett had reminded her the world was exotic, full of feelings and tastes, colors and sounds. She felt alive, and she stood here demanding he not offer her that life anymore. She was nothing but a hot mess.

"Fine." He moved around the hulking counter as if he'd had no intention of touching her. "I wouldn't want to be known as a man who pushes his affections on a woman, but let's be fair. A touch for a touch seems a good rule. That puts the ball in your court."

"Fine." Lana wanted to touch him already, to smooth away the misery etched behind his sardonic smile. Resisting, she tempered her harsh stance. "And if you still want to separate business from pleasure and go out as friends once in a while, I'm willing to agree—friends."

A warm smile replaced his frown. "I'd like that. We've got about another hour before lunch. Can you think of anything else we need to do?" She nodded, and he spun around to face the empty storefront. "Can't you just see the store full of cheerful people having fun playing on the water in one of the cleanest rivers in Missouri?"

"I actually can. I always had so much fun playing down at the riverbank." Lana was relieved by the change of subject. She felt like a hypocrite. "You could hardly pry me out of the water my entire childhood."

"I saw you, you know." Garrett was meandering around the room, looking at the view from different windows, contemplating space. Lana did not know what he meant. She waited to see if he would elaborate. He turned and met her eyes, the tall desk a gulf between them. "Playing in the water, always dancing about, chatting to yourself. Your hair hung down your back, a golden mane on a ray of sunshine, so skinny and happy. I think I knew then we'd meet, but I wasn't staying long. I'd been ill that summer, the only summer I didn't stay year-round at the academy. My grandparents pled for me to stay here." He looked down, toeing at the rough-hewn authentic floorboards. "I never forgot you."

"I remember you, too. You could have said hello. Clearly, we were supposed to meet. You were going to need to hire me to make your resort a reality. I'm good at this crap. It's what I do." She leaned over the counter, her eyes seeking something deep in his. "You're going to have to trust me a little. Have you given much thought to how many people you'll have to hire for just a base crew? People that you'll need year-round... And what you'll do with them in the slow season?"

"A little, but I plan to go with the flow..." Garrett met her gaze, and she knew he saw right through her. She was testing him.

"I hope to hire people who might not otherwise be able to find a job, people who need a job in the summer like school employees, high school students, that kind of thing." Garrett leaned back against a windowsill, his hands behind him. "Depending on the fate of the bar and grill," he winked at her, "I'll need a few full-time employees there. For the campground, I'll rent cabins all year, so I'll offer a few special events through the winter. I'll be needing someone with good customer service skills here for booking and someone to oversee the guests' needs. What do you think?" He whispered as if an on-stage aside to her, "Feel free to correct me, babe."

"No. Sounds like you've been thinking it through. We can work on it, anyway." She had yet to ask about his wedding plans, and she was calling herself a coward when he brought up her homestead again.

"I know it's not a good time to ask again, but have you given any more thought to my offer? If I owned the mill, I could market freshly milled flour to tourists. They'd watch a demonstration, then fork over double what the flour was worth after they watch it be milled. Heck, I could even hold contests for people to have bake-offs for prizes and profit using our flour...."

Lana grimaced, knowing he would bring this up sometime... she wasn't ready. She flexed, steeling her spine. "To be honest, I intended to go by yesterday and decide. The fire—so much of what I have left is there now—I don't see any way I could sell it right now. The joke you made—about me living there? Where else am I going to stay for the next three months? I lived in the only apartment building in Riverbend Falls. After this, I'm leaving, so it wouldn't make sense to rent a house."

She leaned her head onto her fingers, pushing against them to feel the pressure of life, then continued. "I never opened your offer." She looked at him shyly. "After lunch, how about we walk down together? I haven't been there in years, and once I face it, maybe I can think of something to help you out."

Garrett nodded. "Wow, thanks. I'd be glad to go with you." He glanced at his cell phone, checking the time. "Speaking of lunch, we'd better get to the lodge or they might eat without us."

Lana looked around at what they'd accomplished together. Instead of arguing, they'd debated on locations, supplies. Progress. "Sure. Even after a big breakfast, I've worked up an appetite. I have to admit, I'm excited. Thanks for having Tad and I. This will be a tough year for him. He misses his boys terribly."

The warm sunshine melted the snow into a muddy path across the grounds, and Lana carefully avoided the mud. How anyone could have worn pants with such a large bell at the ankle was beyond her. She had to use both hands to hold the jeans up out of the muck. By the time they'd arrived at the lodge, Lana had wet ankles. "Until we go shopping, you'd better drive us down the road, rather than walking. I'll be a mud monster."

Garrett laughed. "I'll drive, though you're just as cute covered in mud."

Emily was arranging an oak buffet with a meat and cheese tray, bread and cracker trays, and a vegetable tray. Set among the serving dishes patterned in red was a huge silver tray piled high with single serving desserts; pumpkin, raspberry, and cherry cheesecake cups, fruit cups made with gelatin and heavy cream, several batches of homemade cookies. The fabulous smell of honey-baked ham filled the air, and Lana's tummy rumbled with anticipation despite her hearty appetite at breakfast.

"Merry Christmas, kids." Emily turned, gifting them both with a warm hug. "Tad arrived a bit ago. He's in the dining room with Jasper. Ya'll head in and visit. The ham will be ready in about twenty minutes."

"Okay," said Garrett, as he scooped up three cookies on his way past the dessert tray. Both women watched as he passed into the next room, Emily with an indulgent smile Lana hoped wasn't mirrored on her face.

She noticed as he passed through the doorway that an elegant dining room table was arranged. Pretty red and green votive candles glowed around the dining room in small crystal candleholders. To complete the magic, several sprigs of mistletoe tied with silver bows hung about the room.

Lana lingered and chose a carrot stick to try the dip. "Miss Emily, I'm grateful to be here. Your home is absolutely lovely. How can I help?"

"Everything's nearly done, honey. This is my last Christmas here, and I wanted it to be special. With you kids here, it is exactly what I hoped for." Emily wiped her hands on the floral apron tied at her waist. "Go relax. It seems Garrett means to work you to death, even on a holiday. He's a bit of a bulldog. Be sure you don't let him push you around."

Lana snorted. "Not a chance." No way would she let him push her around. "I don't take orders very well, as he's been noticing."

"Good for you, honey. I knew you were the one when I first saw you together." Emily patted her cheek fondly. "Now go relax while you have a chance."

After eating, they gathered around the tree, and Lana was shocked to find a few gifts for her, even for Tad. "How did you...? I didn't bring gifts."

"It's okay, honey. Considering the situation, you certainly wouldn't. I keep a few things around, just in case of visitors. Nothing big." Emily patted her white coif pleasantly, though not a hair was out of place.

Slippers. Everyone got slippers from Emily, and oddly enough, the cute ones Lana received had little frogs on them, putting her to mind of her favorite "thinking" pajamas that were no more. Tad gave her a new organizer. Even Garrett got her a gift, but she didn't believe she could accept it. Her heart thudded as she unwrapped it and realized it was from Mrs. Bunsen's jewelry store. As she fought with herself about whether to open it, she decided she would open it and give it back.

The long black satin box held a skillfully twisted silver and pearl bracelet, spaced by moon-shaped alexandrite and moonstone. It was stunning. She held it up, wondering how he could have known her birthstones. She hadn't told him. The strand complimented her in every way. It was perfect. As she slipped it onto her wrist, he reached over to help with the clasp, and heat lingered where his fingertips brushed her wrist.

"Merry Christmas," he said, and she could see the joy of giving in his eyes. He was a perfect gentleman. A smart, smooth, gorgeous guy with that dark-haired, blue-eyed sex appeal he had perfected who wasn't being completely up front with her. Oh, why did he have to be so likable? And mysterious...

After they'd sang carols and drank eggnog, Tad went back to his new abode to call his boys, and Lana and Garrett headed up the road to look over her property. Lana's contentedness from watching Garrett's excitement at the whole Christmas event faded into dread as they got out of his vehicle. She looked past the mill to the large house nestled against the river, showing the passage of years, looking as ancient as Lana felt. Her Mom would never fill the kitchen with the smell of baking pies, her dad would never fish off the back porch, chortling heartily when he caught a fish. "Betty, get out the frying pan. There'll be good eatin' tonight."

She tried not to picture her family not living there anymore, and maybe look through Garrett's eyes, try to see his vision. People would come to see the mill. It could be operational easy enough, even just for demonstrations. They would look to the left of the rambling old building and see...

Lana imagined herself in her room, listening to her parents' arguments drift up the stairwell. "Lana's out of control" or "It's that pack she runs with. They're a bad influence."

Her vision got blurry when she remembered that last night... her folks had been dressing for the Wilcox's New Year's party. Lana was to spend the night at Kat's house, Jaime, too. Her parents had been happy, not fighting. Her mom had looked so beautiful, her dad so obviously in love with her. "Be careful tonight," her mom had said. "Stay out of trouble," Dad said, but he'd patted her head affectionately.

She'd driven off in the practical little hatchback she'd received for her sixteenth birthday. The girls lied about staying at Kat's and went down to the river. The weather was unseasonably warm for the last day of the year. They'd brought gear and firewood, liquor, a little weed. Tears welled up in her eyes as her dad's words filled her thoughts, and she flinched when Garrett touched her shoulder.

"Lana, think back to a happy time. Tell me about it."

"I..." she bit her lip, almost drawing blood. "I... was mostly always happy."

"Then what's wrong?" He prompted her, turning her away from the view. The river flowed sluggishly behind the buildings, the back eddies rigid with an icy froth, but the river moving on, like always.

"I feel like I let them down." Lana looked into his eyes and accepted the strength he was offering her. "There was hardly any fighting until I was about fifteen. Then I started getting in trouble. I didn't mean to, y'know, we were just having fun. My Dad disapproved of Jaime, claimed she was too wild. Her Dad was in the military and she'd been everywhere, moving around to bunches of schools. She wasn't wild. Just experienced, and me and Kat loved her for it. Maybe a little wild, but we were so bored by this dinky little town..." she trailed off, gazing back up at the stone structure.

She imagined them all singing Christmas carols around the hearth—just a week before the house never heard a song again.

"It would make a good restaurant." She thought of how her mother had loved to cook, a gene she herself hadn't inherited, and the double oven her father had bought her for an anniversary gift one year. "The kitchen's... well..." The keys were burning a hole in her pocket. "Since we're here, we might as well check it out." She hesitated, "I don't know about selling it though, Garrett, it's been in my family a long time, and somehow, I think it might not be right for me to sell it."

"Let's not worry about that just now. Let's just go take a peek." He took her hand, leading her toward the mill building first. "So tell me what you know about how this operation worked?"

They locked up the two-story building she'd grown up in, her mother had grown up in... and Lana knew she would never sell it. Despite her dread, they'd browsed the musty house, and the furniture was all still there, covered in sheets by some thoughtful soul. Their sneaker tracks in the dust were the only signs of life on the old hardwood floors. Instead of the emptiness she'd feared, she sensed her parents' love, and it felt like she'd come home.

She wouldn't be able to give Garrett what he wanted, but while they'd been wandering around the mill building, she'd had an idea, and it only seemed to grow as she looked around her house, knowing she was going to move in, make it her own. The mill had three floors and was pretty close to the same floor space, and the distance between the house and mill was enough that tourists would not disrupt her privacy much. Now, how could she convince Garrett?

Straight. That's how she handled everything, so why mince words now? She ambled back across the expanse of lawn, back toward the mill.

"I was thinking..." Glancing at him out of the corner of her eye, she wanted to kiss him. He looked giddy with pleasure, and she knew he hoped she was about to agree to sell. "Well. I never opened your offer, so I don't know how much you were offering for the property package, but I'm wondering if we can make a deal."

He looked at her, and she had his full attention. "What kind of deal?"

"I found the plans on your desk, so I roughly saw your intentions for the properties, but I was thinking..." she unlocked the mill building again, and led him into the dusty darkness a second time, with a different mission, "the floor plan is about the same. The kitchen renovations might be more costly since you'd be starting from scratch, but with the money you save not buying my house, I think it could work." She pointed down the long, wide hall.

"Look how much more room you'd have for the kitchen here, if we just modified it to suit, and you were willing to serve bar food and the upscale cuisine from the same kitchen, instead of in two separate buildings. The grain rooms on this floor could be converted into fabulous dining rooms, enough to seat about forty. We can convert the entire lower level into the bar and ship bar food down from here."

Garrett was looking around, those wiggly eyebrows doing that thing she'd come to recognize as considering. He walked to a service door, glanced through a dusty window out over the river below. "If we put a deck here, we could seat outdoors in nice weather..." He turned to Lana. "You're saying you would be willing to sell me this piece and help me put it together?"

"That's what I'm saying. You could keep the mill operational still, maybe just for demonstrations, and the tourists would already be in the building. This piece here borders right up to what you plan to buy from Tad, and if we shave an acre or two off on this side, you could even put your boat takeout here, right before the dam. People could sit on the deck, watch the waterfall, and wait for their parties to come off the river…"

"How much do you want for it?" Garrett looked excited, and Lana was pleased to have possibly made a real compromise.

"I need enough to pay back taxes and do minor restorations on the house. I… I'll be moving into it. I feel…" When they'd walked through, she'd felt a flicker of excitement at making it her own she couldn't explain. "It makes sense, so for now, if you agree to my price, we'll be neighbors."

"I'm speechless, babe, and that rarely happens to me. I watched your face in there," he nodded his head toward the other building, "and I knew I was lost. You were so alive in there. This is more than I expected." Garrett pushed back the lock of hair that had fallen in his eye as he got more animated. "This is perfect. Better. Are you sure?"

Lana smiled, genuinely pleased by his excitement. "I'm sure. We have to go shopping tomorrow. We'll stop in and visit my dad's lawyer. I never mailed the paperwork yesterday, so I might as well hand deliver it, and take care of this business, too. I'll make some lists tonight. We can negotiate a number tomorrow before we talk to him. Sound good?"

He lifted her off her feet, spinning her through the air, raising quite a dust. "All right! We're on our way." He put her down, but didn't remove his arms. The closeness subtly shifted from friendly to sexy, and Lana was surprised by his lips on hers, then kissed him greedily, wishing he'd lay her in the dust and get rid of the ache that had lodged in her middle since the first time his mouth touched hers.

Instead, he broke away, looking around. "Together, we can do this."

Chapter 11

It was time to go to bed, so Lana climbed restlessly onto the treadmill. She was wearing the gown Emily had lent her to sleep in, and she shed it so she could lose herself in the run without the hem tripping her up. She realized she was still wearing the bracelet and slipped it off as well, placing it back in the box. Lana knew she would treasure the gift forever.

Despite her misgivings about accepting it, she wouldn't give it back, knowing it was so much more valuable than just a bracelet to her. It was the first thoughtful gift any man except her dad had ever given her, and it suited her perfectly.

As she ran, her brain refused to shut off, and she contemplated her current situation. It was crazy. A man she had to work with shows up mysteriously at her Christmas party and doesn't reveal who he is, manipulating her—however innocently, contracting her services, getting her to like him. A few days later, she's enmeshed in his life, from personal to business. She knew in advance he would screw up every scrap of organization she'd managed in her life. And she was falling for him.

At the dance, when she didn't want him to let her go, she had been afraid. It hardly felt real, but since Garrett walked into her life mere days ago, most everything felt different. She felt passion. Stimulation. It made her nervous because it was such a heady feeling. Truthfully, she mostly felt confused around him.

Lana was scheduled to work with him for three months. That meant New Year's Eve, Valentines, St. Patrick's Day, then she'd have to leave him to his own devices for Memorial Day opening, Fourth of July, Labor Day... He would need someone competent to help him through the summer. She could design his copy for him, but who could they get that could pull off all the complicated maneuvers of opening a business? She couldn't think of anyone.

"Shall we head into town? I want to start with the lawyer first. I made us an appointment for 9:30. Would you believe he was eager to speak with us?" Lana grinned at Garrett, feeling a mixture of sheepishness and excitement. "Tad will meet us there too, so we can get everything taken care of all at once. Ready?"

She ran fingers through her hair nervously and handed him an envelope. It was a beautiful morning. The sun was warming the earth, and most of the snow had melted in yesterday's sunshine. The rest would likely melt off by noon. "There are two figures in there. The first, what I feel the Mill would be worth to the highest bidder, which of course, I haven't verified. The second figure is what I would sell it to you for if you guarantee to maintain its historic value. It should remain available to any who want to see it, so it seems to me it's a prime location for your enterprise—if you can incorporate change tastefully—which I think you will. I'd rather you accepted the second offer, but it's up to you."

"I'll take the second offer," he replied, then he opened the envelope and glanced at the numbers. "Interesting that you never looked at my original offer. That still baffles me."

"Well, get used to it. I have a long history of being baffling, and I don't mean to change now. I am what I am." Why did it bother her if she baffled him? He really messed with her.

"I thought after the lawyer, we could hit a few shops around town. We could go to Springfield, but if you want to fit in around here, it might behoove you to shop around here."

"I didn't see a mall in town... Are there really places to shop for clothing?" Garrett's disbelieving look had her grinning mischievously. She'd fix him just right. There wasn't really much in the way of men's clothing...

There was a dollar store and a good second-hand store that carried some clothing, and two shops for ladies, though Lana always avoided Cynthia's House of Designs. Everything in her dress shop was overpriced. A few women in town desired the designer dresses she carried, but Lana put little stock in labels. She preferred functionality. Lana and Kat often joked about Cynthia buying her own dresses and not worrying about generating income—her store was simply a house of gossip.

She would do her shopping at Renee's and the dollar store, and she would take Garrett to Hank's Hitchin' Post. He could pick out some work jeans and shirts from the small selection Hank kept in the back of the store for ranchers and farmers. That should suit Mr. Armani. Practically, though, he could build rapport. Until Hank could find a buyer for his business, Garrett would likely send a lot his way.

"Oh yeah. No worries."

They parked just up the road from Reed Agency, and Lana glanced longingly at the safety of the building, but promised herself to stay on mission. Tad's vehicle was parked in the lot behind Mr. Peabody's legal office, and Lana was pleased everything had been agreed upon. She would do what she came to do and then move on.

The meeting with the lawyer went smooth and quick. Apparently, being the only lawyer in town had given the bow tie wearing fellow the inside scoop. Tad had brought Lana's paperwork and the probate case was settled with much less fuss than Garrett expected. Apparently, all it lacked was the formality of her signature. Separate contracts for the sale of the two pieces of land and the Grist Mill building were drawn up and signed, officially making Garrett the new owner.

Lana and Tad were pleased with the checks Garrett had written them, and though it was a chunk of money, he'd anticipated it, and he couldn't think of two people he'd rather have paid it to. Tad had accompanied them to Hank's Hitchin'

Post store to pick up supplies for his place.

He tried not to show his surprise when Lana led him to a stack of unstylish jeans and work shirts in random sizes. He quickly got into the game and selected several pairs, adding flannels and white cotton tees to the pile. Hank had rewarded his purchases with a hearty handshake and a welcome to Riverbend Falls.

His playful companion quickly shopped for herself and added the purchases to his in the backseat. Several boxes from the store called Renee's and about a dozen bags from the dollar store, mostly full of sensible socks and underwear. He also spied several bags of cleaning supplies. She intended to move into her house as soon as she could get it cleaned up. He'd thoroughly enjoyed watching her shop, and could easily imagine the two of them doing weekly shopping together.

"What will you wear to my grandparents' New Year's party?"

Lana looked at Garrett, surprise clear on her face. "I don't go. I..., well, I just don't."

Garrett shook his head. His Gran said everyone in town attended and that it was nearly as big of a shindig as the Christmas dance the week before. "Well, you'll be my date, surely?" He immediately wished he could take the words back.

"I will not be your date. We will not be dating! Why do you keep messing with me, anyway?" Lana's tone was angry, and Garrett hated he couldn't seem to keep his foot out of his mouth around her. "Anyway," she added, "now's as good a time as any. What are your wedding plans?"

"My what?" Garrett was floored. If she was a mind reader, he was in real trouble. He'd decided yesterday the only way to get what he wanted from Lana was to marry her. Then they could spend all their time together. It would be great. He was going back to see Mrs. Bunsen at the jewelry store and pick up the ring set she'd showed him when she sold him the bracelet.

There was no way Lana would say yes to his proposal right now. He was going to get her relaxed New Year's Eve and ask her romantically. He was sure he'd need things like roses, champagne, his hot tub. He was a long way from getting her there just yet. It would ruin things if she had guessed, because he knew she would shoot him down. "What makes you think I've been planning anything?"

"I saw the note on your desk. If you're getting married and you're just looking for some last fling, you better be straight with me right now."

Her face was red, and she looked like she might cry, but Garrett couldn't contain his laugh, which only seemed to make her madder. "Boy, you didn't miss a thing, did you?" He laughed again and brushed that infernal cowlick out of his eye. He needed a haircut. "I haven't gotten very far on those plans because it depended on whether you would sell to me, but after I establish the basics, I thought we could offer wedding packages. Don't you think overlooking the river would be an ideal place for a couple to be married?"

She looked confused. "Wedding packages?"

"Yeah, you know, like get married and honeymoon in the same place? We sell them a cake, rent them chairs, a gazebo, a cabin... that sort of thing. What do you think?"

"So you're not getting married?"

"Not that I know of." Yet. He'd almost married the wrong girl once. Fate had intervened to give him this chance with the right girl.

Lana frowned and started back down the sidewalk, passing a classy looking dress shop without glancing at it. Garrett stopped and looked in the window. "I'd like you to attend New Year's Eve, and I think you'd look lovely in that." He gestured at a lavender strapless dress displayed in the window, a half jacket resting on the shoulders. The mannequin didn't do it justice, but Lana's lithe body would. She finally stopped and walked back to where he stood, her eyes hesitant. He smiled. He'd win her hand yet.

Lana hesitated, hating the fact nearly everything he said or did filled her with hesitation. Usually she was matter of fact, and it was driving her nuts that he so effectively upset her defenses. "If I came, I could just borrow something from Kat. She should be home soon..." Lana wondered what that gown cost. No doubt Cynthia would have it marked up double what it was worth, and it was exquisite. A L'Wren Scott design, unless Lana missed her guess. "She has a simple black dress that's nice."

"Black isn't your color, sunshine." Garrett took her hand and pulled her into the shop.

The pet names were too much. They were supposed to be maintaining formalities, and they were staring at dresses, shopping together... Good grief. He was so wonderful, it was frustrating. She had noticed Garrett caught the eye of several women in town, and despite Lana's presence, most all the ladies flirted shamelessly with him. Lana couldn't tell if he'd already met so many women in town or if he was just friendly to everyone who spoke to him, especially the beautiful women.

Lana wondered if she were misreading him. Perhaps he was just being friendly to her, too. Her dating skills were rusty, but it would make more sense than him being interested in her romantically. She was plain and awkward. She wasn't ugly, of course, but she was far from the sophisticated women who seemed so interested in catching his attention. The more she thought about it, the more it concerned her. She was out of her league here. He was every girl's dream guy, and she knew he knew it.

"Penny for your thoughts, babe."

"Sorry," said Lana. "There's not a chance I would reveal thoughts like these for a mere penny. Look, I can't afford anything that fancy, nor do I need it. I'm a practical girl."

"Let me be impractical for you. I want to buy this for you, a thank you for all your help to get me outfitted." He nudged her to the counter, and she gave way slowly. "You've gone above and beyond for me, and I know my Gran would want you to feel like the belle of the ball. Consider a dress a meager trade for the huge favor you're doing me."

"I don't think I'm comfortable with that. With your tricky maneuvering, you're technically my boss, for now, and I don't think you should buy me party dresses." Lana was certain she needed to maintain control of this situation. She hadn't realized just a little shopping could seem so intimate.

Garrett scowled, his eyes darkening a shade. "Boss," he muttered. "You need a dress for the party, and this is the dress. No more arguments," he said. "Let's see if it's your size." And she was at the counter, his fascinating gaze sparkling over her, top to toe... He was enchanting, and she was in over her head. He was just fun! She was enjoying herself so much she couldn't bear to walk away. Every moment spent in the company of this impulsive imp was infused with magic and delight, and she liked it too much. Dadgummit it.

"Is this really necessary?" It was the hundredth time she'd asked as she modeled dresses while Garrett pretended indecision. The gal who owned the store claimed the dress in the window to be one-of-a-kind and she'd resisted taking her display apart, but Garrett convinced her.

Lana was playing dress up for him while the shopkeeper undressed the mannequin. Lana was fun, he thought as he watched her, the way she approached everything with delight. So fresh and genuine compared to the superficial women he had dated in the past, and the difference was invigorating.

She came back in the dress from the window and Garrett could barely keep his racing libido in check. As she spun around, the pale orchid dress seemed to hold her body tightly in all the right places, and flounced enough to be fun. "Perfect," he said. "Now for some shoes."

"Garrett, this gown is way too fancy for me. It's not even realistic. The only reason I tried it on was because Cynthia went through so much trouble. I think she's frustrated with me."

"I'll make it worth her while. You look beautiful. You'd never choose that for yourself. That's why it's perfect, and not too fancy." Garrett nodded his head appreciatively. "Believe me, you look top shelf, babe."

"But, Garrett..." Lana protested again.

He held up his hand to forestall her argument and said, "Do you hate it?"

"No," said Lana quietly, smoothing her hand down her slim

waistline, wrapped delicately in the shimmering satin.

"Then what we need now are some matching shoes." Garrett glanced at his cell, checking the time. "I have something else I want to pick up. If I leave you for a bit, will you pick out some shoes that go with the dress—whatever else you want—a bag or something?"

"Some shoes, only. Heaven knows I have nothing to go with this dress."

"And don't give that gal too bad a time. She's jealous of you, that's all. Take the high road." Garrett smiled and took Lana's hand, spun her once, and gave a low whistle. "Save your hard times for me. I'm enjoying arguing our affairs."

"You're obnoxious." Lana giggled. "And you're touching me. You aren't supposed to, whether or not I like it."

He tugged her to him, unable to resist, and touched her lips lightly with his. "You could always change the rules, goddess."

He was totally aroused by the way her heart was slamming around inside her chest, her playful giggling stifled by a heated gasp. She pulled away from him, and Garrett knew the moment she was gone, she'd retreated again. How was he going to convince her to come out of her shell and stay with him?

He left her with a very shocked looking saleslady, staring at Lana as if she'd grown an extra head, and went to run his errand. Just a few more details to prep for his plan. He needed a swimsuit to get her into the hot tub—he'd seen the perfect one at Renee's. She'd already have the purchase bagged. He just needed to dart in and collect it on the way back to the jewelry store.

When Garrett asked Lana to marry him, he wanted everything to be perfect. He had selected a ring that had stones similar to that of the bracelet he gave her for Christmas, with a syncing gold band that would join the ring when ultimate promises were made. She liked the bracelet, and an engagement ring would convince her he was serious about wanting her in his life.

When leaving the jeweler with the small satin box in hand, he was conflicted by doubt, a rare experience. What if she said no? She hadn't given him a lot of hope for their future. How could he put himself on the line completely if she hadn't even offered him any reason to think she would accept him?

He put the thought aside. He would ask her to stay with him, marry him, be his partner in everything. She was competent and exquisite. How could he not try to hold on to that one-of-a-kind girl forever? Garrett knew a good deal when he saw it, and Lana Stone was a good deal. Could he convince her, though? The woman was as stubborn as her last name. He'd already availed all of his charm to her and he just seemed to keep messing up, not saying the right thing. He had to admit, he wasn't as smooth with women as he'd thought he was, at least not this woman.

Lana was so supportive of him, expecting so little for herself. He knew he would be miserable if she wouldn't be his girl. He consoled himself, knowing the evening he planned at his place would win her over if anything could. He had to win her heart, and soon, because he was about to be too busy to have time.

When Garrett returned to pick her up from the dress store, she was arguing with the saleslady, trying to pay for shoes and a handbag separately. The handbag was perfect with the dress, but she didn't want Garrett to pay for it.

"I trust you aren't giving this gal a hard time, right Lana?" Garrett spoke from behind her. "I left her instructions that whatever you wanted, I wanted to get you."

The saleslady smiled adoringly at Garrett. "Everything is in order, Mr. Wilcox, just as you requested. I'll just bill this to your card, then."

Lana pouted. "Do you always get your way, Garrett?"

"So far," he replied. "Are you ready?"

She started to gather up the packages when Garrett beat her to it, taking the boxes from her.

"Anything else I can do for you?" The sales gal was batting her eyes at him, but Lana beat him to the response.

"I appreciate your help, Cynthia. Sorry to be so much trouble."

"No trouble, Lana," said Cynthia, but Garrett sensed undercurrents. "Have a nice day. Mr. Wilcox, now don't be a stranger."

On the way out the door, Garrett poked Lana in the ribs. "She won't be looking forward to waiting on you again."

"I'm sorry, we've known each other a long time and haven't been great friends," said Lana. "I'm really not used to being spoiled like this."

"We'll have to change that, won't we?" Garrett said, hoping he'd get the chance to spoil her indefinitely.

Lana was looking out the window dreamily as they headed back to the river with their purchases from the day, and Garrett contemplated her profile. How did one go about convincing someone to marry you when it seemed she had yet to decide if she liked you? He knew he could make her happy... How to convince her of it? He could start charming her with dinner tonight, a private dinner in his cabin, say to celebrate the land sale...

As he pulled his glance back to the road, Garrett knew they were in trouble.

A large supply delivery truck was barreling toward them in their lane with not much time to avoid it. Garrett thought fast, deciding from the path of the vehicle that the driver would not correct in time, and he quickly jerked the vehicle into the other lane, honking his horn. Lana screamed, the sound muffled by her head being buried in her lap.

He looked into the rearview mirror and saw the driver correct, narrowly avoiding rolling his truck. The truck slowed to a stop. They had avoided the possibly fatal accident. He looked for a place to pull over, afraid for Lana.

Jumping out of the rig, he rushed to her side and yanked open the door. Carefully reaching in, he tried to get a handle on the situation. He couldn't see anything wrong, but Lana was shaking like a leaf, terrified. He put his arms around her, held her, and just waited for her to catch her breath.

She could not shove her fear back into the box it broke out of. Her worst nightmare came to life. And ended differently. Lana knew when she saw the truck rushing at them they were going to die. This wasn't a dream. Instead, they were safely on the side of the road. The sun was shining, and she was being held close in the comfort of Garrett's arms. She was safe. Maybe she was dreaming.

"We're still alive?"

"I wasn't planning to let you get away from me that easily." Garrett's smile was concerned, but his tone was light. He put his hands on the side of her face and gently kissed her nose. "Are you okay? I thought you were hurt..." He was looking at her arms and legs, apparently reassuring himself she wasn't wounded.

"We were almost in a wreck, and I thought... my parents died in a car wreck about a mile up the road. I didn't." Lana pulled herself together. Garrett helped her endure and survive her worst fear. The thought empowered her, making her brave. "I don't like to talk about it." She kissed his mouth generously, melding into his lips as much for reassurance that she was alive as the sheer pleasure of it. She leaned back reluctantly. "I'm sure you don't need to hear—"

"Tell me," Garrett said.

Lana paused, considering the man in front of her. He seemed to understand what she needed, even though it had little to do with what she thought she wanted. "Let's make a deal," she said. "I'll tell you about it if you tell me why you don't talk about your parents. Deal?"

Garrett scowled. "You drive a hard bargain, but I want to know everything about you, so I'm willing to trade information. I'll cook you a nice dinner tonight at my place, and we'll talk."

"I guess I'm pretty anxious to find out just how good a cook you are." She wrinkled her nose. "At your place? Alone?"

"You'll be fine. I promise not to take you wantonly, however tempting that might sound." Garrett chuckled. "Let's get back. Are you sure you're okay?"

She settled back in the passenger seat and strapped in, muttering mostly to herself. "I'm okay. I'm ready. For what exactly? I don't know, but I'm ready."

Chapter 12

Lana dressed herself in her new black silk pantsuit with a critical eye on the mirror. The top was simple, with long straight lines, blousing out into a flare at the wrist. The bottoms were similar, the legs flared. She decided she liked the flare after all, and when she'd seen this outfit on the rack at Renee's, she'd selected it without hesitation. A new style. So many changes since Garrett danced into her life with his crazy pandemonium. She slipped on the bracelet he'd given her for Christmas and took a deep breath.

She felt like a virgin, nervous about the first time. She knew she looked good. Her hair was swept up from her face, and she wore a new pair of fake pearl studs in her lobes. She walked to the door when he knocked, gave a nervous tug on her shirt, wondering if it fit too tightly, then faked a confident smile and opened the door.

Garrett wore new clothes as well. A navy and royal checked flannel layered over a white tee, and jeans wrapped around his narrow hips invitingly, stretching provocatively across the zipper area. She needed to put a stop to these random thoughts. It's just that he jumbled her up with his nearness. She looked him over, wanting him.

"Well, are you ready to brave my cooking?"

Lana laughed nervously and nodded. She didn't know why her tongue seemed incapable of forming words, and she drew another calming breath. Rather than going back inside and hiding under the covers for three months, she stepped onto the porch and pulled the door shut behind her. As they walked through the hedge leading to his place, she heard barking again. "Do you have dogs?"

"One of Pap's beagles just had a litter of pups over there in the kennel." He pointed to a very plush doghouse surrounded by a generously fenced yard. In the near darkness, Lana could see two beagles, and... puppies! She high-stepped it over and knelt to pet them, pushing her slender fingers through the fence. Roly-poly furballs bounced over to lick her while Mom and Dad beagle just looked on from their palatial beds. "They usually have run of the place, but Gran doesn't allow the puppies inside, so when the hounds get a notion to have a litter, they come out to Ma Dame's palace, as Pap calls it. So you like dogs?"

"Mm-hmm." She stood, brushing puppy fur off her fingers, then sniffing them for that sweet scent of puppy breath before she breathed a delighted sigh. The view beyond the evergreen hedge was its own wonderland. Garrett's cabin was like hers, maybe larger, but instead of a view of the river, his place nestled into the wilderness. Behind the cabin, there were miles of treetops dropping into crevasses in the land, providing an amazing view of a sunset that colored the sky like a watercolor, full of deep pinks, oranges and blues. And it was very private. She wouldn't have even known there was anything beyond the hedge if Emily hadn't mentioned it. "Wow, great place."

"I'm still settling in, but it's home." He swung the door open and invited her in. It smelled like heaven with tomato sauce and garlic.

She gave him an appreciative glance. "I love Italian."

"It's my lasagna," he said. "It's not exactly a traditional recipe, but it's my favorite, so I can kind of... whip it up. I figured since you order like I do, this was safe."

"Really? You made lasagna in three hours? It's on my top ten list." She gave him an encouraging smile while remembering her own attempt last year. It had taken closer to five hours from prep to bake. Then the noodles were hard, the sauce runny. Another plus for the man.

"Oh, good. Make yourself comfortable. I need to finish throwing together a salad." He went to the kitchen and returned a bit later with a dishtowel over his shoulder and two glasses of deep red wine. "Sweet girl," he said, bowing slightly and handing her a glass. "Dinner will be about twenty minutes. If you want music, my CD stack is inside that cabinet."

He disappeared back into his kitchen area and Lana shamelessly admired the view of his perfect 10 rear end wrapped in denim. Yum. She perused his CDs, noting they had similar tastes in music and selected a classic Tom Petty. Then she wandered around the space he'd so quickly made his home. She smiled smugly when she opened a drawer in a curio and found it filled to the hilt with chips and candy bars. So, he wasn't totally perfect. He'd teased her mercilessly about putting away large amounts of french fries.

She poked her head into his bedroom, embarrassed by the giant bed covered in cotton navy sheets and a handmade quilt, mostly because it was still rumpled from his sleep, and she could imagine him in it. Apparently, he wasn't a bed maker. Or a user of hangers, she thought as she noted expensive suits and shirts thrown carelessly over chair backs. She was surprised by the vast collection of exercise equipment in the room. A stair stepper, free weights and a bench, a treadmill… No wonder he had such a muscular body. She'd been imagining what it would be like to spend the summer with him when he would no doubt traipse around shirtless. She started to back out and pull the door closed, but she bumped into Garrett, who had walked up behind her.

"Want a closer look?" he whispered, his hot breath next to her ear, sending delicious warm tingles all down her body.

Lana tried to invent a clever response that might help her locate some dignity, rather than the weak-kneed swoon she was in danger of giving in to because of his delicious closeness. When she turned to make her smart remark, Garrett was a picture of innocence.

"I can tell by your toned body and the way you move that you work out religiously." He looked genuine. "Want to check out my equipment?"

Lana responded playfully. "How long until we eat? I'm starving."

Garrett lifted one brow slowly, a sly smile curving his lips at the sexual undertone of their banter, but he was behaving. "Your salad is on the table, the lasagna is cooling. Shall we dine, babe?"

Lana followed Garrett into the dining area, pleased by the quiet elegance of his table. He kindly pulled back her chair, then snapped a lighter to bring the squat white candle in the center of the table to life.

When he sat across from her, he looked serious, but just began poking at his salad. The two ate companionably while Garrett told her about the restaurants he'd worked in, how he'd gone to France to study under a great chef and met a woman he almost married but luckily hadn't, how he'd often been given kitchen duty at the academy where he went to school which was how he chose culinary, how his parents traveled extensively, his father a military liaison, his mother the devoted wife.

Lana was surprised at the wistful tone the conversation took when he spoke of his parents, but he seemed proud of his father's work.

They cleared the plates from the tasty triple-layer lasagna, did dishes together, and were now seated back at the little table with a slice of raspberry cheesecake to share. She had her coffee in hand, trying to think while Garrett stared at her intently, waiting for an answer.

Lana swallowed the urge to get up and run. "I'm afraid of a lot of things, I guess. I'm afraid of spending too much time with you, Garrett Wilcox." Lana flashed him a rueful smile.

"Don't you like spending time with me?" Garrett reached across the table and picked up her other hand. The feeling of his enclosing her smaller hand was comforting. He said nothing, just waited, watching. Lana wanted to pull her hand away, but the heat spreading throughout her body was like a love potion, and she felt in tune with Garrett, wanting to share with him as he'd shared with her.

"I enjoy being with you, it's just... I'm not looking for anyone to spend time with. Truthfully, until I met you, I didn't think I could settle with anyone, ever. There's something about you that makes a girl feel more... spirited, I guess. I find myself being with you easily. I mean, who wouldn't like you? You're... well, I'm sure you know..." Lana trailed off, feeling like she admitted to him he was the man of her dreams. "Your turn. What's the real story with your folks?" Time to redirect.

He pulled his hand away, rubbed his eyes. "Nothing really. They stopped visiting me regularly at the academy when I was eight, except for ceremonial functions where it looked bad on them if they didn't come. We aren't that concerned about making up for lost time. They go their way, I go mine. It's simple, and the way I prefer it. We don't agree about things."

Garrett's eyes studied her seriously, despite his light tone. He wasn't planning to be redirected. "Since I've believed you might hit me in the head for arranging for us to work together, I'm rather relieved you've decided I'm not too bad of a fellow." He took a small bite of cheesecake then—she'd almost eaten the entire piece—and added, "As far as everyone liking me, life is too short to worry about all of that. The important thing right now is that we like each other. Do we agree on that, at least?"

Lana took the last bit of cheesecake off the plate, popped it in her mouth, and took her time chewing. She eyed Garrett interestedly, not knowing where he was going with this, but curious. "I suppose it would make our jobs easier if we knew where we stood with each other. But I don't see how talking about something we can't do anything about can change anything. I wouldn't get involved with a client, and despite how we keep kissing, our situation is even more complicated..."

"What makes you think there might be a situation we can't do anything about? Besides, communication creates opportunities to grow." Garrett leaned forward. "I would guess in your line of business you must agree with that?"

"Certainly," said Lana, "but I haven't told you about the jinx either. Every man in my family as far back as my great great grandpa has either gotten divorced—or been killed. Including my folks. So you can see why being with a Stone is dangerous. If I get involved in a relationship, you can see it's destined to fail. That's the main reason I don't indulge in love. It hurts."

"Are you serious? A smart girl believing in superstition like that?"

"Of course I'm serious. You don't think I'd make that up?" Lana shook her head, subconsciously fingering the scar on her jaw. "Stone women are bad luck."

"Well, now if you married me, you'd be a Wilcox, and I'm making up a new superstition. You're a good luck charm." Garrett smiled nervously at the obvious panic brought on by the word marriage. She'd almost choked, as if to say, marriage? Not for this girl.

"You're making fun of me," she said.

"Maybe you should try letting us work together, instead of against each other. You might be surprised at how much more lucky life can be," Garrett suggested softly. "Do you ever dream of me?"

"Yes. No. That was a sneak attack." Lana laughed, seemingly glad for the change of subject, whatever it was. "And you're mannerly in my dreams."

"Mannerly, huh?" Garrett laughed too, and for the moment their laughter shared the same space. Lana felt an intense closeness with the man across from her. "Are you trying to ruin my reputation? Are you suggesting I don't mind my manners?"

"Uh huh."

He stood up and helped Lana out of her chair. When she was standing, he pulled her up against him. "In that case, I'll get to work on being a little more mannerly another day." His mouth pressed against hers for a light hot kiss that left her head whirling.

She didn't cringe, even let herself indulge in the aftermath. She smiled at Garrett, a warm flush in her cheeks. "I don't know what I'm going to do with you," Lana said, then murmured quietly, "but I'm afraid I'm going to enjoy it." He led her to the living room, and her nervousness returned as she seemed to wonder what they would do now?

Garrett stopped in front of his entertainment center and paused. "Would you like to watch a movie or take a spin around my dance floor?" He gestured toward the cleared space in the living room.

"Movie, definitely," Lana said without pausing. She remembered clearly the feeling of his arms wrapped around her on the dance floor. The memory made her cheeks hot, but luckily Garrett was fiddling with the DVD player with his back to her and didn't notice. She went over to the couch and sat a careful distance from where she suspected he might sit. He showed no such care in choosing a spot after he put the movie in, and spread out across the rest of the couch, his head propped in his hand inches from her lap.

Lana wasn't sure what movie they were watching, though Garrett said it was a popular romantic comedy. She was wary, prepared to fend off his advances. After about an hour, she got disgruntled. He was completely interested in the movie, unaffected by their proximity. The movie ended, and Lana could not remember one bit of it. She'd been wrapped up in his stimulating scent and closeness.

They stood up, face to face, and Lana was pleased to see the hungry light in his eyes, thinking it affected him after all. He reached up and pushed back a piece of hair that had escaped her updo, tucked it behind her ear, and she closed her eyes, anticipating his kiss. She wanted it, wouldn't fight it. She could feel his moist breath on her lips, the wintergreen candy a promise of the invigorating flavor of his mouth.

Then he was gone. She opened her eyes in surprise. He'd crossed to the entertainment center to fool around with the movie.

"I'd offer to put another movie in," Garrett's voice was strained, "but I don't think I could honor my promise to be a gentleman since I'm not doing so hot with the no touching rule."

"Oh, Garrett," Lana said, and started to cross over to him, then berated herself. What was she doing? If she gave in, she would never be the same. Could she give a man everything, knowing she would be left alone, empty inside? The curse... She stopped mid-stride, uncertain, knowing she wanted to, but not knowing if she could. Garrett took her hesitation as a rebuff. His voice was gruff. "I'll walk you back, then."

As she slipped her shoes on, she cursed herself for a fool. She wanted him, no matter what it cost her. She would take the memories he gave her, cherish them forever. She just wouldn't let him too close. Maybe Tad got the only dose of curse meant for her generation. Maybe despite their differences...

Garrett was waiting by the door and she took her time crossing the room to where he stood. "I'm not ready to leave yet unless you want me to," she said, stretching up to meet his lips. She nipped his lower lip hesitantly, playfully.

"Oh, Lana," Garrett groaned, wrapping his arms around her. "I don't want you to go." He crushed her mouth in a hard kiss, and Lana felt engulfed with passionate heat. Her tongue flicked his lower lip, urging him to share his mouth with her. She no longer felt hesitant. Everything felt right. Their mouths passionately mated, and Lana lost her sense of self, longing to join with her dark knight, knowing the certain fate, but uncaring.

Lana's hands were in Garrett's hair, pulling him even closer into her, and their bodies matched the meld of their mouths. Lana felt his masculine hardness against her abdomen, and was rewarded with a shiver that set her whole body on fire.

"Lana, we have to talk," Garrett murmured, when their lips parted.

"Shh. No more talking... I just want to be with you," she said silkily.

Garrett bent his head down and gently left a trail of kisses from her mouth to her earlobe. He nibbled on a tiny corner of the lobe, making her body ripple with electricity. His fingers were gently kneading the small of her back and Lana wished her clothes were gone so she could be closer to him. Her fear of the future was blighted by the need of now. "Oh, Garrett, I want you."

Garrett pushed her away, gently, but determined. "We can't do this, Lana, not like this. I'm not that kind of guy. Not like this," he repeated, taking another step back. "I think we better call it a night, after all. Let me walk you."

Lana felt shocked, then hurt. Did he think she was that kind of girl? What did he mean, not like this? She was no expert, but it seemed the perfect time for her. She was ready to give him everything, for just a moment in time, and now the chance to share something magic with him would likely be gone forever. She would not let her guard down again. Had she indeed been mistaken about what he felt? What if he was not interested in her, maybe playing a game? She felt a door snap shut inside her. A chill filled places that had flared with tingly vibrations moments ago.

Lana drew from a reserve of strength and affected her haughtiest voice. "I remember the way, thank you. I prefer to walk alone, to be left alone," she said. Carrying her jacket, she pushed out the door past Garrett, mindless of the cool night air.

"Baby, don't be mad. You don't understand…"

Lana left him talking to her back. She understood all right, she had walked straight into a grand mess. She hurried back to her own little place, wondering how on earth she would find the strength to finish this job.

What possessed her to offer herself to him, knowing it would be a one-night stand? Why did he change his mind? He was the one coming on strong. When she responded, he turned off like a faucet. She did not know what he was thinking—nor did she want to—she reminded herself. Apparently, the challenge wore off when she was willing.

Forget men anyway, especially interesting men like Garrett. She sank down on her bed with hot tears sparking at her eyelids and pulled the covers over her head. "Oh well." Lana mumbled the mantra that helped her through many nights, "I'll worry about it tomorrow." It didn't work this time, though. Was it obvious to him she was an amateur? He was surely accustomed to more sophisticated women, so why would he want her?

"Ugh," she cried aloud in frustration.

She got up from the bed, drying her tears, and began stretching before warming up to full impact aerobics. Exercise burned away rejection before in her life, and it would work again. She worked out for an hour, until her body ached with fatigue, yet still she felt the sting.

Garrett had pulled back from Lana, aware of the fact if he hadn't stopped, it would have been next to impossible after another of her passionate kisses. He was so aroused by her intensity, he could have lost control of himself and taken her right there in the doorway. Something told him despite the change in Lana's personality, she was not the kind of girl who could have uncommitted sex.

A girl with fire like that could convince him to offer her anything, and he wanted to. Now she had withdrawn back into that prickly shell. Too much raw emotion had lain bare between them, the mood suddenly broken. There was no chance of preserving any dignity, and Lana would not appreciate her vulnerability.

Man, he was crazy about her. It wouldn't be smart to have her close all the time if he couldn't have her. It would be slow torture. He would have to have her. Convince her somehow to want him. He sat down hard and put his head in his hands. He'd fallen for her, she despised him, and they had dynamite sexual chemistry. "Bloody blast," he muttered, "what a mess.

Chapter 13

The next few days had flown by awkwardly as Lana worked side by side with Garrett, setting up multiple computer stations with minimal conversation. They seemed to be getting along okay, but they hadn't really talked. Lana had taken it in stride. It was technical work, and they needed to pay attention. But he had been distant, had something else on his mind.

Whatever was budding had not bloomed, and she had tossed and turned through the night.

Today was the day she was moving in to her place. She had taken the day off, and while Garrett insisted he would help, she was impatient to get started. When he didn't appear with breakfast for the first time in a few days, she packed her meager belongings and told herself it was just as well. Leaving here was a good idea. She wouldn't be able to stand being so near Garrett on New Year's Eve tomorrow night. It was a night she always spent alone, and this year would be no different. She felt saddened by a loss she had yet to accept.

She hoped the thrill of making her old home hers would fulfill the promise of excitement she'd felt walking through. Kat would be home soon to fill a little of the void. She'd convert one of her new empty bedrooms into a workout room, get a free weight bench for herself, and a brand-new pile of how-to books... Between Garrett's projects at the resort and her own, she'd be able to put the man himself out of her mind. That would help her find wherever she put her normal sense and sensibilities.

She reached up to rub the tense muscles in her neck and reassured herself returning to a regular schedule would help. She would force Vivian to let her back into her office, find Garrett a competent secretary and stay out of his path while the shame of rejection faded.

There was a knock on the door. Finally, Lana thought, feeling relieved. If she could apologize for being so prickly and indecisive, she could make amends and leave with a clear conscience. When she opened the door, I surprised her to see her brother.

"Hey kiddo. Seems the bad luck just keeps piling up. I ran into Garrett outside the health clinic in town. Jasper suffered a heart attack last night. Everyone's there now maintaining vigil while the doctor decides just how bad the attack was. Garrett was going to call you, but I told him I'd be happy to run out here and let you know, give you a ride into town if you want to join them. You haven't picked up your car yet, have you?" Tad looked at her curiously, clearly surprised by the detail. "Well, want a ride?"

"Definitely." She gestured at the three small bags, gave a quick glance around the cabin she'd cleaned last night where she'd grown so much in such a short time. "Let's just drop these off at the old house on the way." She grabbed her things, dropped them inside her new door, and prepared herself to be strong as they took the short drive into town.

When she arrived in the waiting room, she was distressed by the lack of hope on faces she loved. Emily's face was wet with tears, and Garrett's eyes were closed, his face pale, his head resting against the wall.

Emily started when she saw Lana. "Oh, Lana, you didn't have to come, but I'm so glad you're here. Doc Abrams was just here. He said it was just a little scare, Jasper will be fine. He's going to have to make some lifestyle changes, but he's going to be fine."

Garrett looked up and his haggard expression worried her. He tried to smile, but it wasn't much of one. He slid over a seat so Lana could sit in between Emily and himself, and Lana quickly moved into the spot. Tad stood a minute, shifting uncomfortably until he excused himself, mentioning he'd be back later. He'd never been comfortable with sickness or grief.

She rested her hand on Garrett's thigh for a moment, giving him a reassuring squeeze, then turned to Emily and embraced her. Emily cried softly, and Lana held her, letting her cry. After a few moments, Emily pulled back and dabbed her lined face with a linen handkerchief.

"I don't mean to burden you, Lana. I was just so frightened. I'm not ready for Jasper to die." She began crying again.

"Don't worry, Emily, you'll get him whipped right back into shape." Lana patted Emily's shoulder. "Let's look on the bright side. Everything's going to be fine."

"Right, I should think more positively. That's what Jasper would want me to do, and I love him so much," said Emily, wiping her eyes again. "I have details to handle. I'll cancel our party tomorrow night. I couldn't possibly focus on it, though Jasper will be disappointed." Her voice faltered, then she pulled herself together and dabbed at her tears again. "It's his favorite party of the year. Everyone comes, locals, customers, and friends. Right now, though, all I can think about is how scared I was when I thought he might be... It's too bad about the party. I wish there was some way to still have it. I know it would raise his spirits. I just feel as if all the energy has been drained right out of me."

Lana made an impulsive decision. "If it's what you want, and what Jasper would want, I can handle the arrangements and play hostess for you. Garrett will help, won't you?" Lana asked, turning to Garrett.

He looked surprised. "I didn't think you'd want anything to do with the party."

Lana smiled kindly at him. "Right now, it seems I'm needed."

Then she added, as it occurred to her Garrett might not want her help, "If I wouldn't be imposing."

"You're needed, Lana."

"Dear girl," Emily said, "I could get used to having you around. Because the party is an annual event, most everything is arranged. It shouldn't be too much work, but I'm still afraid it would put you out too much. You've had so much trouble of your own. I know New Year's is hard for you since your parents passed on. But Jasper would want the party to go on. I can—"

Lana cut in, "No, you take care of yourself, and Jasper. With Garrett's help, I'll take care of everything else. I have plenty of experience planning parties for the locals, so I'm sure it'll be fine. It's too bad I haven't come to one of these parties before, but you know," she glanced at Emily shyly, "first I was too young, then... well, we'll make everything just perfect for Jasper." Lana reached out to catch both of their hands in hers, gave a tight squeeze, and sent up a silent prayer for Jasper's health.

A little later, the doctor came into the waiting room, looking tired. "They've moved Jasper to a room, if you'd like to visit briefly. He will, I have to reiterate, need to make lifestyle changes if he doesn't want to find himself back here again, or worse, being flown to a larger hospital for bypass surgery. His heart is weakened. I've discussed this with him, but he seems a bit stubborn."

"Yes, doctor, I'd like to visit with him, please. I'll talk sense into him," said Emily. "Garrett, why don't you come back and reassure yourself he's going to be all right, then go home and get some rest. It's been a long day already and not even noon yet." Emily turned to Lana, kissed her on the cheek. "Thank you for coming and thank you for taking time out of your busy life to make a couple of old people happy." Tears glistened in her bright eyes as she patted Lana's hand and left to follow the doctor.

"Do you want to come or wait here for me?" Garrett asked gently, his firm hand resting on the small of her back.

"I'll wait for you." Lana was rewarded with a genuine smile that shone in his sweet blue eyes.

"Thank you. I'll be back in a few." He followed Emily down the short hallway.

Lana sat back in the chair and wondered if she could stay in his close company for much longer and still fight these growing feelings for him. She felt a surge of panic, but knew it was way too late now. The feelings began the moment he held her in his arms at the Christmas dance, and had only intensified as the days hurried by. She called Tad to let him know she would ride with Garrett.

When Garrett stepped into the hospital room behind his Gran, he stood to the side of the bed. His Pap's appearance was ragged. There was a tube hooked up to him, machines in the room beeping continually, reassuringly, and Garrett touched his hand. It was warm, and Jasper's eyes opened clear and strong.

"My boy, can you get me out of here? Sick people around here. I'm liable to catch something."

Garrett grinned. After finding the man he respected most lying on the floor in a pool of spilt milk last night, he'd been considering how short and full of surprises life could be. "I'm afraid the doctor has put Gran in charge of looking out for you, Pap, so it's out of my hands." He glanced at her, wondering how she was taking his appearance. She was looking back at him with a speculative look, a confidence in her carriage not clear an hour ago. She looked at her husband.

"I was so frightened to lose you, Jasper, but we have another chance, and I for one plan to take advantage of our new opportunity," Emily said.

"I'm so glad you're all right," said Garrett. "Now I'll leave you to get lined out." He patted his Pap's hand, reassured again by the warmth. He'd been so cold last night. Emily followed him out of the room, into the hallway.

"He's a belligerent old man," Emily said fondly. "Listen, I could tell this morning something was wrong between you and Lana. Promise me you won't let this chance pass you by. You take care of that girl, make her happy. Use this party to show her how charming and worthwhile you are. I'll watch over him."

Emily patted her grandson's arm gently.

Garrett smiled at her, treasuring her. "You can be devious when you want, Gran. Thanks, I don't aim to let her go."

Emily smiled back at her grandson proudly. "Nothing would make your Pap and I happier. She needs a family. She's been so lonely, holding herself above the fray all these years. He likes her, you know, he can't wait to be a great grandpa. Go home, get some rest, then help Lana with the party. You'll find all of my notes on the credenza in the kitchen. Go on, now, we'll be fine. I'll call you and let you know what time we'll be home. The doctor didn't seem to think there was any reason to keep him overnight, as long as he takes it easy."

When Garrett returned to where Lana was waiting, he told her he was pleased she'd offered to hostess. He had knocked on her door late last night, hoping to clear the air between them, but she hadn't answered and he'd gone to the lodge to see if Emily was still awake.

He'd needed to talk. That was when he found his grandfather lying on the kitchen floor. He'd called the clinic, arranged for Doc Abrams to meet them, then loaded Jasper into his backseat, freaked that he might lose two people he cared about.

When Lana placed her hand on his thigh this morning, he felt her compassion, her caring, and the male stirrings in him made him want to sweep her up and kiss her senseless. Now he would take her home, and work on how to get her to stay permanently. When they got there, Lana was sweet and concerned, and insisted on seeing him back to his cabin to help him settle in. Garrett was too exhausted to argue, and he let her in, flopping down on his couch.

"Are you in the mood for a light meal?" she asked, starting for his kitchen.

"Yes," Garrett answered. "Look, Lana, I want to explain about the other night…"

"Please don't. I shouldn't have put you in such an awkward position. You really have been a gentleman, mostly playing by the rules and all…"

"Blast it, Lana, the only thing awkward about the position you put me in was it wasn't lying down," Garrett growled. "There's no doubt I want you, desperately in fact, but..."

"Please Garrett, don't explain. I'm an adult, and I know things can be complicated. The situation got out of control, and I'm glad you stopped it because I felt out of control."

Even if she had liked the feeling. "Now listen, you've had a horrible shock. Let's get some food in you. Then you can lie down for a few hours until Emily calls. Now my cooking is much more rudimentary than yours, so you'll have to bear with me," she joked, attempting humor.

Garrett stared at the woman, frustrated. She organized everything into some logical little compartment that fit neatly into her organized life. He did as he was told, mostly because he was too tired to argue, but vowed to make a place for himself in her life, whether or not it fit into her plans, and really soon. She was driving him mad with her on and off switch. The sexual frustration was palpable. She would be his wife, then her volatility would mellow. He wolfed the cheese omelet and toast she put in front of him, and in short order, pushed his plate back.

Garrett stood and asked, "Come lay down with me for a few minutes? Just until I fall asleep."

Lana hesitated, hard. "For a few minutes," she relented, "but only because I think you're tired enough I could win a fight if you try anything." She followed him to his bedroom.

He stripped off his clothes down to his boxer shorts in nothing flat. Lana's breath hitched at the back of her throat, her heart fluttering wildly against her ribcage. He stretched out across the bed and pulled back the covers, motioning her to get in. She slowly took off her shoes, but left herself completely dressed in soft velour jogging pants and the light T-shirt she'd been wearing when Tad knocked on her door.

"I'm only going to stay a few minutes. I have work to do in the old place, since I know you'll recover your bearings soon enough, and put me to work..."

Garrett grunted and reached up. Grabbing her hand, he gently pulled her down next to him. He slung his arm around her, resting against her, and his breathing pattern changed to one of sleep in the space of a minute.

Lana willed herself to push his arm off and get up, but she really didn't want to move from his comforting embrace. She drifted off to a restful sleep, the scent of him filling her every breath, and woke an hour later with Garrett's arm still slung over her possessively. Lana grinned crazily at the comfort the simple gesture brought her. She was in over her head. She knew it, and she loved it.

She climbed out of the bed and decided a brisk walk would clear her head. She stepped out the back door and discovered the back porch was surrounded by a screened in deck that housed a hot tub. Beyond that, she found a walking trail that slipped off down the hill into the trees. Intrigued, she followed it. It wasn't terribly muddy, and the late afternoon sunlight cast dappled patterns through the tree branches. All but the evergreens seemed impatient for spring.

As she walked along, she reflected on the events that led to now, and how she was changed because of them. She considered her loving relationship with her parents, their death, and how she had retreated into herself and latched on to the notion of the jinx to help her stay out of trouble, the kind that meant putting her heart on the line.

Her parents had loved each other, and they'd loved her, so why had she convinced herself love was so wrong? She knew she felt she'd betrayed them when she'd lied, leading to her arrest, and she'd internalized the feeling, as if anyone who loved her would be betrayed...

She was so busy trying to bury her own grief, she realized she had been punishing herself for a long time, and had never really grieved for them.

Tad was definitely changed by the loss. He had lived in denial also, having made a life with a woman Lana knew was superficial. He'd seemed happy enough at first, especially once their first son was born. It had hurt her to know he was in a loveless marriage, though, and she'd rarely visited.

She mulled over the change in him since he'd been back, and after visiting with him, she could tell he healed somehow. He had come home to make a life for himself, to face whatever he'd been avoiding here. His enthusiasm had been catching, and it was satisfying to know he was helping himself, despite his problems.

She disturbed a ring-tailed hawk that flew from a tree where it'd been resting on a high branch, only to stop in another tree before taking wing again and heading in the direction of the ever-flowing river. Such a majestic bird, free of constraints. Squirrels chattered at her, probably protecting their winter stash of nuts, and she smiled at their antics.

She realized she too was helping herself, facing things now, and the result was a happiness she hadn't felt in some time. Determined to examine her emotions deeper, she considered her relationship with Garrett. He made her smile, flutter, tremble with fury, and crave the taste of his lower lip. She felt good when she was with him.

Jasper and Emily made her feel welcome, and Lana knew she wanted to be included in that kind of happiness, make that kind of life for herself. Garrett seemed to fight his own demons, ironically where his folks were concerned. Lana realized she'd walked quite a distance further than she intended, but the path seemed to stretch on for miles. The trail needed worn in, and Lana was struck by the desire to jog on this path every morning instead of the little track in the park. She was growing. Oddly, she had to lose all she had found comforting to do so. The breeze was fresh and invigorating, and she tasted freedom in the air.

As she turned back toward Garrett's cabin, she sent up silent thanks for Jasper's incident being minor, instead of deadly. She had put on a strong front when she went to the clinic, hoping to be a comfort to those closest to Jasper, but was upset herself. There had been no chance for her folks. The thought of such a wonderfully vibrant man dying brought a tangible stab of fear.

What if it was Garrett, and he'd died? What if she'd begged

him to take her heart? As if she would catch herself begging. The realization that she was terrified of any kind of intimacy that would make her vulnerable was a fear she knew she must conquer. If she never opened her heart to anyone, young or old, she would cheat herself of the depth of feelings she felt the past few weeks. Not all good feelings, granted, but she'd been *feeling*!

Her life would be here in Riverbend Falls. She would not run. Since they helped her, she would help the Wilcox's as much as possible. Emily would need a few days to readjust to Jasper's new situation. Garrett had a lot of work ahead of him, and he would need her help. While he was confusing her, she had to feel maybe he was confused, too.

He could have any kind of girl he wanted. Maybe he liked Lana, maybe even wanted to be more than friends, but she couldn't imagine him settling down with a girl like her. She knew she frustrated him. She could not hold her tongue when he ordered her about. She was always arguing. Perhaps he preferred docile women. He'd said his own mother played the perfect wife. A man like him would like a big bosom, a soft curvy body, and a sweet tongue, putting her sassy skinny self out of the running. The woman would be a trophy wife. Lana laughed at herself, knowing she longed to be wanted by him.

Her muscled body could never be soft and voluptuous. She was not. Even so, he seemed to like her. It was a contradiction. She wanted to share his bed, take for herself memories she would treasure, knowing he helped her grow past the borders she rigidly maintained. Now she was alive. She headed back toward Garrett's cabin, feeling light-hearted and happy, despite knowing it would all end. For Stone women, it always did. When he'd mentioned marriage, he'd quickly laughed it off. That spoke volumes.

As Lana came into view of the cabin, her heart gave a leap to see Garrett standing on the back porch, brooding into a mug of coffee. Her stomach gave a tug, and she burst out laughing at the petulant sulk in his stormy eyes. He was wearing a pair of blue jeans, and despite the cool air, nothing else. Lana wished the pulling in her stomach did not feel so much like yearning.

"I wondered where you disappeared to," he said when she got close. "Are you laughing at me?" He was still sulking.

"Just clearing my head." Lana surprised both of them by planting a soft lingering kiss on his mouth. "Coffee smells good. Is there another cup?"

Garrett stared at Lana, arousal in his eyes. "I'll fix you one. Did you enjoy your hike? That's some nature trail, isn't it?"

"I loved it. I thought I might jog on it soon, see how much farther it goes."

"I like you planning my backyard into your future."

"Has Emily called yet?"

"Just a few minutes ago. She said Pap was restless, and they'd be discharged within the next few hours. Do you want to come with me to pick them up?" They went inside and Garrett poured her a cup of coffee.

"I'd love to." Her hand began tingling in reaction to Garrett's brief touch when he passed her the cup.

"Gran said the doctor is worried the party might be too much excitement for him, but he just laughed, said he never heard of a party not being good for a person. She assured the doctor the party preparations were in expert hands and she would dedicate all of her time to making sure he behaved himself."

"I bet she will," said Lana, smiling. "She intends to get him well, then take advantage of the fact they have more time together. She's an awesome woman."

"She also mentioned my parents were coming, that they'd be here tomorrow, maybe tonight," Garrett muttered, scowling. "I suppose my Mother wants to be where the action is."

Lana sensed his aggravation, but didn't understand it. "I'm sure they're just concerned about Jasper. You should look forward to their visit. Maybe you can mend fences with them." Maybe after Lana met them, she could help. She groaned inwardly at the fact she was so caught up in this man she was concerned about solving his personal issues. She let the inevitable be. Now that she was in love with him and knew it, she might as well try to make him as happy as possible before she went back to her old life.

"Well, let's knock out a few errands before we pick them up. Should we go up to the lodge and find Em's notes so we can get started?" Lana forced her mind to a safer topic.

Garrett swept in close, his eyes hooded with desire. "I'd rather stay here with you and get something started." He touched his lips to her nose in a sweet gesture that made Lana feel weak in the knees, then he took her hand and headed out toward the lodge. "But I suppose we should run the errands, so Gran can take it easy."

Chapter 14

When they walked in the back door, they heard a commotion at the front door. "Garrett, Garrett, where are you? I need help with these bags."

"Ugh." He rolled his eyes. Lana bent to clean up milk spilt the night before. "My parents are here already."

Garrett started out the kitchen door and stopped with a grunt when a tall, curvy blond pushed through the swinging kitchen door. "Oh mon, ami! Garrett, I've missed you so!"

Unless Lana was mistaken, there was no way this French beauty could be his mother. She was Lana's age. The way she wrapped herself around Garrett, kissing his cheeks, wasn't the least bit maternal.

"Felice." Garrett stood there, seeming quite surprised. "What are you doing here?"

"Your Mother invited me to the party, darling. You must take me shopping to find something to wear. We passed this quaint little boutique on the way in. Certainly, I'll be able to find something simple enough for a rustic little to-do, yes?" Her gaze traveled past him to Lana, still kneeling with the damp cloth, and her eyes narrowed slightly. "You are the maid? Madame Wilcox would like assistance with the baggage." She dismissed Lana, returning her attentions to Garrett. "I was afraid there were no staff here. So how have you been, mi amor?"

"Why are you here?" he asked, his voice hard.

"Let's go sit down, darling. Your Mother asked me to help with the party. You will be needing a hostess, no?"

"No."

Lana was ready to split. The maid? If her career took any more nosedives, she was going to freak. Less than a month ago, she'd been an up-and-coming in the advertising world. The entrance made by "Madame Wilcox," in Lana's opinion, sent things from bad to worse.

She was also beautiful, though perhaps with the help of a plastic surgeon, more so than the naturally exotic look of Miss Frenchie. Lana's hand was on the doorknob, almost out, when Garrett's mother spoke in a voice accustomed to being obeyed. "You, girl. Please carry our bags to the guest house."

"The guest houses are occupied, Mother. And Lana is not…"

"Actually, I cleaned it just this morning. It is vacant, ma'am."

Garrett turned to look at her, finally distracted from staring at Miss Ooh la la, several emotions stirring in his eyes, and the look that remained made her more nervous than his mother's voice. He smiled at her—oh so wicked—and faced his mother. "I'd like you to meet my girlfriend, Lana Stone. Emily has asked for her expertise in handling the party, so you'll simply have to relax and try to enjoy yourself, Mother. Now why don't we get you ladies settled? Father can help me carry your bags. Where is he?"

Both women were staring at Lana as if she might need stepped on. "I'm not really his girlfriend."

"Yes, she is. She's staying with me until we finish her house repairs. So, ladies, unless you want me to be angry at you for insulting my girlfriend, I recommend we find Father, and get you settled. I'm sure you all want to see Jasper right off, and it may be a few hours before he's released. Lana," he looked at her, a cold blue steel shining in his eyes. "I'll be back, then we'll go. Emily left you a note or two on the credenza."

"I don't actually need any help, Garrett. It's okay with me

if you want to take them to pick up Jasper and Emily." She wanted to be anywhere but here, feeling these feelings. Anger, humiliation, jealousy, lust. He stood up for her. She couldn't believe it. Who was this girl that had him acting crazy? Someone special to him. Once. She was sure.

He ignored her, herding the women back out the front door.

She found everything she needed to plan for the party outlined in well-prepared lists Emily left, but as she looked over the notes, genius struck her. What if they used this event to showcase Garrett's resort plans to the town? She could charm the town council, gather suppliers for the goods, put out feelers for summer laborers all with one bold presentation. Emily would be delighted with the idea. She whipped out her phone and texted Vivian to let her know she was coming in. She would start by transforming the ground floor. There was work to do.

Lana gave him an ultimatum. He would drop her at her car, and she'd run errands, starting with Reed Agency. He would trust her to handle everything. If he did, she'd fire up the locals and customers who attended with rockin' resort anticipation tomorrow night. If not, she'd sell him down the river to get her way, leave him at the mercy of the ladies quietly fuming about Garrett's rudeness, and go clean her house. The ladies were likely plotting already, the visit obviously geared toward Garrett rather than Jasper.

If he let her have her way, she'd meet him back at his place tonight and fill him in on all the details. He'd sleep on the couch. He grumbled. He conceded. Lana felt he had his hands plenty full of women without her adding to the count in the hen house with hens waiting to pluck at the perceived weakling's tail feathers.

He dropped her at the Widow Donovan's, where it had been helpful to garage her car, and helpful to the Widow Donovan to have a little rent coming in for the space. She unlocked her hatchback and backed out from the garage, heading around the corner to the office. She waved cheerfully as Garrett drove away with his own to do list. Free at last. For now.

She'd have to get in the groove to accomplish what she intended so quickly. She checked in with Viv first.

"Lana, how are you? Bless your heart, sweetie. What can I do to help?"

"Believe it or not, things are moving right along. At the moment, I need my office and the drafting room. I'm going to—"

"Hello… Vivian, Lana? Are ya'll back there?"

Kat appeared in the doorway, and Lana hugged her best friend desperately. "You're home early. Wonderful!" A minor miracle. "I need your help with entertainment."

"My great aunts yapping Yorkies were getting on my nerves. Thought I'd come on home, make my resolutions here." She ran a hand through long black hair that settled in silky straight locks as if she hadn't disturbed it. "I saw your car out front, thought it was weird, then noticed your apartment was gone. I high-tailed it back to find out what happened."

"I'll explain everything later. So you don't have plans for tomorrow yet?"

Kat looked at her curiously. "I might go on out to the Wilcox party. Since you went all hermit on me, that's what I do if I'm in town."

"Perfect, you're hired for karaoke tomorrow night."

It was late when Lana arrived at Garrett's. There was a bright moon, and she tried not to draw any attention to herself on the way to his cabin. The lights were blazing at both the lodge and the cabin she'd recently vacated. She felt like there were eyes everywhere. Too bad, though. She was excited to show Garrett what she'd accomplished, although she shouldn't have agreed to stay in his bed tonight. Why on God's green earth had she agreed to sleep here? Quite improper. And exciting. Sort of. Still just business.

Lana had known what she had to do when she first reclaimed her car. Despite wanting to honor her contract to make things easier for Garrett, she'd realized it would only make it harder on her. There was no future between her and Garrett, despite his fancy words and her foolish daydreams. There was nothing wrong with a little harmless flirting, and Lana was convinced that was all that was going on between them. If she stayed beyond tomorrow, she would have no excuse. She had obligations. If not, she would create them.

The door opened, saving her the trouble of knocking. Garrett was waiting for her. Oh, this was a mistake. He was angry, she could tell. Judging by the storm evident in his eyes, she shouldn't be so happy. What he was mad about, she hadn't a clue. He left the door open and retreated inside, leaving her to follow. He had showered and changed, and was wearing jeans and a tee shirt, his feet bare. He looked untouchable.

"Why is it women think they have to get what they want?" Garrett looked at her, sat on his couch, stood. She just watched him, still unsure what he was about. No way he could know what she'd done today. And if he was mad because of it, they would have to go rounds. He walked to his kitchen and came back with two longneck beers with the caps already sprung and handed her one. With a long pull on his own, he slumped back on the couch. He patted at the seat next to him once, the barest invitation. Despairing at his dejected motions, she sat.

"Tell me about your day." Garrett threw his arm along the back of the couch, leaned his head back and closed his eyes. "Please tell me some good news."

Looking at him carefully, Lana decided whatever he was upset about, it wasn't her. That meant maybe her news was still good. "I have everything arranged for tomorrow except some last-minute transport of goods, and approval from you for what I did today."

Garrett didn't move. After a deep breath, he asked, "And tell me, babe, what did you do today?"

Before her answer formed, his expression changed about three times. Need, anger, and frustration were at war with his usual positivity. Even when he settled for a vaguely interested expression, a storm lurked inside him.

Lana became apprehensive about the French girl. She should have seen it coming, but he was the one that made the idiot claim about Lana being his girlfriend. So, was he breaking up with her now, or what? Thank goodness she had taken the day to collect herself. It's not like she was really his girlfriend...

"Show me what you got, Lana. It's been a long day."

"Yeah, yeah. Got too many girlfriends all the sudden, Mr. Wonderful? Putting you in a good mood?" Lana waited for him to scowl at her and turned around the full color posters she'd brought in, complete with now and then laminated pages that overlaid the park.

She leaned them up against the entertainment center for maximum effect. She'd done three, one showing the campground, one a side view of the old mill turned into an elegant dining establishment with a bar on the lower level—complete with the deck he described.

Her best effort was an overview of all the property he owned.

Many years ago, a pilot had taken an aerial photo of their homestead and the surrounding area and sold it to her dad for fifty dollars. Lana had remembered it and found it earlier today. She scanned it in and manipulated the photo into a clever demonstration tool.

The Mill Bar & Grill, his new restaurant site, was close to the intersection of Pine Tree Road that led from town and turned onto River Road. All around the Mill and the homestead were pockets of rugged woods, creating a park like atmosphere. The twelve wooded acres between Lana's home and the campground were the acres he just purchased from Tad, running straight into the slice of land Lana included for The Mill. The canoe takeout and parking would be just past the restaurant.

His campground was the last place on the right, with houses along Old River Road before you headed out to the highway and beyond Riverbend Falls. The other entrance originated from town, where you could drive along the river toward his resort or turn left and drive through Stone's farmland and timber before it ran into the old Hixon place and looped back to the highway.

The river flowed across the page, and she flipped down an additional laminate that put boats on the water, outlining float trip availabilities, prices, and boat options. Then she stood back and waited.

He fought the urge to snap at her simply because his day had been insane since leaving her at her car when she'd ditched him. He'd sensed it as a harbinger of things to come. She'd completely breached the contract she'd signed, albeit with his reluctant permission, and done a fine job. She'd brought to life what had only been a picture in his mind, seen his vision, and turned it into something anyone could see. "It's good."

"Good?"

Obviously, she was like every other female. She wanted more. Man, he couldn't believe his mother had sunk so low as to bring his ex-fiancé here. His mother spoke to him more after he broke off his engagement than she ever had, pestering him for explanations. If Felice hadn't said what happened between them, he didn't intend to, but obviously the little cheat used his silence to integrate herself firmly into his mother's social circle. It had been over two years, for Christ's sake. Talk about a sick puppy. Why had she remained fixed on him when he obviously wasn't what she'd wanted in the first place, to his relief?

She'd cornered him after he settled Jasper in, in a very tense little family gathering that he hoped never to repeat. She had the nerve to say she was getting him back. He told her she was nuts, she should leave, and move on with her life. She'd just smiled her coy fake smile, as if the dare was on. Sick chick. She'd tried to convince him she had no idea why he'd broken off their engagement. It was ridiculous, and he refused to play games with her.

"It's wonderful, Lana. Your talent is outstanding." He was feeling nasty, and he could hear it in his voice. Lana didn't deserve it, not when she'd worked so hard, but Garrett wanted more from her than that. Why did she not love him?

"I've taken care of setting you up media to disperse over the next few months to keep the hype alive after tomorrow night's party." Lana spoke quietly.

"I've talked to several gals around town and secured jellies and baked goods. They've agreed to provide you samples tomorrow, if you agree to sign the contracts to buy their recipes, and provide interested parties with the possibility of a position." She waved her hands at the presentation boards. "The council's coming, all six of them, and I arranged these boards as a special demonstration for them in addition to the opportunity to see your ideas. I even hired an entertainer for tomorrow I think you'll want to use. In short, Garrett, I've done everything I agreed to in a lot less time. I wouldn't feel right about charging you what we agreed upon. I'll even draw you up some notes, explaining what I've done so you can follow along if you feel the need. But I'd rather you just contact me at the office again, if you need me. I'll be staying around, I think."

Garrett stood up abruptly. His tone was carefully devoid of emotion and the emptiness of it shot through Lana like a poison dart. She had asked for it though, and she would carry it through.

"Well, babe, guess that's it." Garrett pushed his hand through his hair, agitation evidenced in the movement. "I'm thrilled with the media you designed, and I'll be sure you get a positive recommendation. You'll get your career advancement and be free to make your escape from my company. Sorry I've been such a drag to be around."

"You haven't been that bad," said Lana. "I just need more room than what you give me. My life is complicated right now and I have a lot to deal with. I've enjoyed working with you."

She'd effectively shut him down, out. He'd been so sure she'd come around.

"Hmph," Garrett snorted, then said more politely. "I apologize, babe, that was unmannerly of me. I remember promising to work on my manners. You deserve an award for the ability to maintain your professionalism. I hope it keeps you warm."

"Garrett, don't be nasty," Lana looked at him, obviously hurt. "We've worked hard and produced a beautiful thing for your company, and that's what we set out to do. Please, don't be angry. I don't know what I'd do if I thought I hurt you. I told you in the beginning I thought it was unreasonable for you to need three months. I'm good at this. It's what I do."

Garrett relaxed and smiled sadly. "You're right, Lana. You never asked for any of this. I'm just tired. I didn't mean to take it out on you. Look, I'm going to lie down. Pap made it home safe. Gran said to thank you, tell you she was excited about the changes."

"It was nothing. I just took what she had laid out and maximized it for the future of your resort," Lana said. "So, will you release me from the contract now that I've taken care of everything?"

Garrett sighed. Outfoxed by a fox. "Certainly. As you wish."

"Oh, thank you. You have no idea how it grates on me to be bossed around." She blushed. "Not that you're horribly bossy, just, oh, never mind."

She was so cute when she blushed.

One more try… "Look, I was wondering, perhaps you consider things differently since you aren't working for me? Maybe you want to try being my woman—"

"I don't think so, Garrett," Lana interrupted. "I was hoping you'd still be my date at the party tomorrow night, though. Uhm, who's Felice?"

"She's history. I'm sorry she's here. If I'd known she was coming, I would have stopped her."

"What are your plans for dealing…"

"Haven't you noticed my plans are to win you over?" Garrett flashed her his charming smile.

"I think we have everything in order then," Lana leaned forward, studying her artwork. "Just a little more elbow grease at The Mill tomorrow, and everything should go smoothly. I'm excited about this."

"I can see it written all over you. You really are good." Garrett glanced back at the boards. "Thanks for all you did to help around here." He sat back down on the couch next to her. "Will you let me help you move in to your place?"

Lana hesitated. "Okay, if you're sure you have time? You could help me move some of the furniture and such..."

"You can have as much of my time as you want." Garrett leaned closer to her, holding her gaze.

"Must you always flirt with me? It makes it terribly difficult to concentrate."

"That is my sole ambition, goddess. To make it as difficult for you to concentrate as you make it for me."

Lana pulled back, looking at the mock up boards again. "That's hardly fair. You engineered me being practically fired from my office so you could have a fancy secretary. You left me no choice."

"Don't be defensive," Garrett said, sliding his arm through hers and drawing them close, face to face. "I like it when you distract me. Until I met you, my life was incomplete. I needed you to come along, so distract me—please."

"So, is that what I am to you?" Lana asked, clearly flustered by his closeness. "A distraction?"

He kissed her then, as he'd wanted to since she first walked through his door. Despite all reason, he still wanted what he wanted, and he wanted her to marry him, make babies, share his life.

He wanted her to wish for him tonight, as much as he would wish for her, as she slept alone in his bed. Her kiss rocked him. Her tongue was provocative, hungry, a complete contrast with the way she talked and acted. She was a total mystery, likely would always seem mysterious to him, but he was willing to spend long years figuring her out.

He dragged his mouth away from the desperate need on her lips. The desire to plunge in despite all of his intentions was powerful, but he shook it off, aware of how desperate he was himself. He longed to touch the length of tightly muscled legs that seemed to climb up her body forever. Wanted to take her clothing off a piece at a time, slowly removing the practical undergarments lucky enough to be wrapping so sweet a girl. Mmm...

These thoughts were only going to get him in trouble. He

shook his head, trying to clear the hot images he'd conjured. "What do you want us to be to each other, Lana?"

She pushed away from him, off the couch, taking her beer. "I don't know. I've never felt so confused. I like you, but I... I just don't know. I need some time to think." She took a long swallow, and it looked like she was trying to drown her own thoughts.

"How much time do you need? You already know what you want. Why fight it? You just refuse to deal with it because you can't catalog the emotion. I want us to hang out together. I want you. Admit you want what I want."

"I can't. It's been hard for me to get this far, and I've done it on my own. I'm independent, and I don't want to change. We're so different. You see things through such a bold perspective, while I'm cautious, I fear we would argue about everything. I like my life the way it was, mostly." She paced the small room. "I worked hard to earn a reputation in my field and I have responsibilities, to myself, to Vivian and the agency—"

"You have a responsibility to us, Lana," Garrett punched his hand into his fist. If this was to be a battle for her heart, he would be as bold as she accused him of being. "We're not so different. We're a balance, just open your eyes. Think about your responsibility to us. You owe me that."

"No." She was so quiet, Garrett felt desperation claw at his gut. She was about to break his heart and she knew it and didn't care. "You employed me, and I have a responsibility to do the best job I can for your company, but I don't owe you anything. I'm sorry if I seem hard, I've really grown to... to like you. I don't want to hurt you, but I've made no secret of the fact I don't feel like I can maintain a relationship."

"Why?" Garrett demanded. "Am I asking too much? I don't believe it. I think you're scared."

"Maybe I'm scared. Maybe you ask too much. When I'm around you, my systems overload. You're too much, Garrett. I'm just not ready."

"Lana, my sweet, how long will you make me wait? How long must I wait for you to look into your own heart so you can see what I see?"

Her cheeks flushed and her green eyes glittered defiantly. "Everything I've learned since we met reinforces that I have to make my own way. I have to stand on my own two feet first, and I'm not ready to give up my heart to the struggles of a relationship. I'm strong enough to go it alone."

She walked to his bedroom door, her voice quivering. She didn't look at him when she spoke, but there was no mistaking her tone. "I'm sorry, Garrett, after tomorrow, all this is over. I've done what you hired me to do. We're finished." She closed the door with a determined thump and Garrett knew it was true. She'd closed him out. With a heavy heart, he lay down his weary body on the couch and closed his eyes. He would not sleep a wink.

Chapter 15

The lies tasted bitter on her tongue and the tears streaming down her cheeks felt like they might never stop. She cried herself to sleep and drifted into a dreamy place where she heard Garrett but couldn't see him. He was calling out his love for her while she moved through the darkness, looking for him. She could smell his fresh breath, his smooth cologne.

Lana sat up in the enormous bed, red digital numbers on the nightstand informing her it was just a few minutes after one in the morning. Something had woken her. She got out of the lonely bed and opened the bedroom door. Garrett was sitting on the couch, staring silently in the low light at the project she'd stretched out in front of the entertainment center.

"Garrett?" Her voice sounded husky with sleep to her own ears. He inclined his head to acknowledge he'd heard her. "Uhm, ya know how we just laid next to each other earlier? Do you think you could come lay down with me, next to me? Just so you'll be more comfortable?" He returned his attention to the layouts without comment. A few minutes later, she returned to the bed, leaving the door open.

Sometime later, she heard him stand, then saw him hesitate at the open door. "Please," she said, and lifted the covers for him to climb under when he approached the bed. Without talking, wearing his jeans, he slid between the covers, lying rigidly.

Ever so slowly, she shifted her body to cuddle him, and laid her hand on his chest. His breathing hitched with her touch, and she stilled, then slowly stroked her fingers over his heart, feeling a matte of soft hair that ran down to his belly button and beyond. Her fingers traced his abdomen muscles, simply drifting back and forth over his stomach, back to his chest. She was getting to know the lines of him, and the hypnotic feel of his skin was firing her passion.

She continued her exploration in the dark, feeling of his features; his eyebrows were soft. She ran her fingers over his scalp, relishing the thick shaggy fur. Her fingers traced over his eyes, nose, to his lips.

He caught her hand there, moving nothing but his hand to hold her own, and he pressed his lips to the sensitive skin of her palm, kissing each of her fingertips, then released her hand, his own dropping heavily back to the mattress.

Her pulse was skittering, her heart fluttering wildly like a caged lark, but the darkness made her bold. The vitality he radiated had her aching for the coupling that would ease their need.

She leaned over him and resumed her touching, sprinkling gentle kisses across his flesh. He moaned softly when her lips opened to kiss his nipple, and her tongue quested out for a taste. Yet, he stopped her when her hand hovered near his zipper.

Without words, he drew her hands to his lips, kissed the fingertips gently again, then ran his hand down her side. He drew her close and offered her his mouth, which she greedily accepted. They lay like that, soft kisses and gentle touches, until they drifted into a light sleep, hands, bodies and legs twined together, until morning light tinged the sky.

She woke at 7:30, staring at the sleeping man next to her, and felt very confused. She wanted to trace the laugh lines, his lips, to dwell in the pleasure he'd given her without even taking his pants off. Something important had happened last night. Maybe they could overcome their differences to find common ground.

At the moment, she was going to take advantage of the

jogging path and clear her head. Though they'd barely slept at all, she felt full of energy. It was going to be a good day, she felt sure. She pulled on some of his sweats, big, but they'd work, and she set out. She jogged a long way before turning and heading back.

When she approached his cabin, the scene before her stole her air. She slowed, wishing it was not too late to turn and run again, to banish the image from her mind.

Standing on his back porch were the forms of an unmistakably taut and delicious Garrett with his hands on the arms of exactly the kind of girl she'd imagined he'd wanted. Lana wished she could blame her inability to breathe on the long run.

Seeing her, Felice stepped out of his arms and walked down the back steps through the little screen door. She tossed her hair in Garrett's direction—perfect hair on a perfect girl—and gave Lana a wave.

"Bonjour! á bientôt!"

Lana had no idea what she'd said, but hated that it sounded so deliciously French. No wonder he hadn't taken his jeans off. He hadn't decided which girl he wanted. Maybe he'd even imagined she was his French girlfriend last night when his hands caressed her—well, that was an impossible thought. No way could he have confused her ugly muscles with Miss Frenchie's curves. Lana's body was a tool to be used to control her emotions.

So much for not wanting him. Her heart was breaking into a million pieces.

She walked up the steps slowly, determined to pretend last night meant nothing to her. She couldn't care less. He was scowling after his friend, but smiled when he looked at her and she swallowed with difficulty.

He was perspiring heavily, sweat sliding down his temples, his mass of black hair sleeked back with the same damp perspiration. Apparently, she'd given them enough time for a proper bump and grind session as well.

"I can't believe the nerve of that woman," Garrett groused, holding his hand out to Lana, scowling at her when she didn't take it. "What? I've had enough of these blasted games. I wake up, you're gone, so I decide to work out. Burn off some steam. Next thing I know that... that woman is standing in my bedroom. You can be assured I was showing her the way out. Don't look at me like that, Lana."

There was an uneasy silence while Lana tried to think of something clever to say. Nothing came to her, and she just looked at him. Last night had been a mistake. She was consumed with willingness to throw caution to the wind, and obviously she shouldn't have been. No. She'd just been a tease. Finally, she said, "You're just a lucky man. Just wait until summer. You'll have plenty more women to choose from. You'll be a real hot ticket around here. We have work to do today. Let's get busy, lover boy."

He grimaced. "For heaven's sake, Lana. Don't close me out. After what we shared last night..."

"A pillow, Garrett. A pillow is what we shared. Today you get what you want. We'll attend the party tonight together, but our work is done. What I do for you from now on is off the clock. Everything is arranged, so let's put on a shiny face, and get everything tight for tonight's unveiling. Friends?" She thrust out her hand. Reluctantly, he studied her with a sardonic smile, as if looking for a trick. He took her hand and pulled her into his arms.

She didn't pull away. Oh no, she was going to enjoy this last day that she and Garrett would play the part of a "couple." It had been his idea to introduce her as his girlfriend, and she'd play it to the hilt, at least anywhere that girl could see them together.

No way was she going to let Miss Frenchie have Garrett easily. Even if Lana couldn't keep him for herself, that chitlin didn't deserve him. A friend wasn't the plan when she woke up next to this man, but it was now, and any friend could see that the woman was no good.

Garrett would always be too impulsive for her, as a case and point. He leaned down and grabbed her legs, then swung her up into his arms. He spun her around, then stopped and placed an arousing kiss on her stubborn but traitorous lips. She wasn't ready to be over him yet. She'd play it out, just for today. Tomorrow she'd deal with the aftermath.

"Good morning, babe." Garrett tried to pretend nothing had happened. "I had the most amazing dream last night, such an exquisite creature you are. A dream come true."

Lana giggled despite herself, shining radiantly in his arms, knowing it, and hating herself for it. "If it isn't Prince Charming, come to steal all the hearts in the land," Lana said, squirming playfully. "Flattery will get you everywhere, sir. Now put me down."

"I plan to begin with you, river goddess, then charm your entire kingdom," Garrett teased in a roguish voice. He set Lana back on the ground, kissed her again soundly, and made a bow. "Join me for coffee, then we can go see how Pap's doing this morning. He asked after you last night, and I know he'll be excited about the work you did for tonight."

Lana's heart was thumping powerfully from the kiss, and she wasn't sure she could breathe right yet, let alone drink coffee. "I think I'll hop a quick shower. You go on ahead, and I'll catch up with you later."

"Will you wear your new dress for me tonight? It's my favorite item of clothing to envision taking you out of."

Lana's heart melted, but she would be strong, guard her heart. She was far from being out of danger.

"Sure, why not? I'll wear the dress, but I have to be clear about last night. Uhm, the stuff we did, we can't do that again. I'm going to pretend to be your girlfriend tonight to help you save face in front of your mother, but I think you should tell the truth. If you're being honest with me about Felice, I think you should be honest with her, too. 'What wicked webs we weave…' Anyway, tonight is my last night here. You'll have to engineer a breakup if you don't come clean."

"If I'm telling the truth?" He narrowed his eyes at her. "Are you saying you don't believe me? I don't give a flip what they think."

"I mean, sure, why wouldn't I believe you? You didn't lie to me, right? Anyway, I'm off to the shower. See ya after a while." She left him smoldering on the porch and went to indulge in a hot shower and her own sullen thoughts.

Garrett was frustrated beyond words, and his determination was mounting. Felice did that on purpose, he believed, knowing how it would look to Lana.

Felice had been up to something, playing him out, but he hadn't caught on to her deviousness at first. She'd teased and goaded, pushing at him until his temper fired. He wouldn't be surprised if she'd been spying on them, and watched Lana leave.

He'd felt her leave the bed, but he'd been reluctant to have it end, so he languished a bit. He should have gone running with her, but he hadn't. Well, she would just have to learn to trust him.

He needed his grandparents' advice. He went to the lodge, then pushed open the swinging door between the family room and kitchen and was glad to find both of them propped in their favorite chairs, relaxing and chatting, with no sign of his parents.

"Good morning. How's the patient this morning? Minding your manners, Pap?" The question put him to mind of Lana dreaming of him being mannerly.

"Impatient is how I am," Jasper grumbled. "I'm out of commission and you kids are flipping tradition on its head. You go invite all my guests to take part in some wild scheme at the Mill, and I don't get to help. I can't even dance with my wife. Doc's orders. Argh!"

"Hah! I'll get you a good view, Pap, where you can watch Gran work her magic on the dance floor with me. Lana set up a spectacular venue yesterday. I can't wait for you to see how she transformed the ground floor."

After throwing herself into cleaning and decorating yesterday morning, Lana had made herself scarce again. She was avoiding him, but Garrett wasn't having any of it. She wouldn't face her feelings if he didn't keep exposing them.

She was a master at dealing with things using a timely and methodical procedure, and love just didn't work that way. You had to feel, and his feelings were sure. They were both deep down that well.

"Normally I would count on you to keep the jackals off my woman, but I suppose this evening, you'll have your own woman troubles, eh? She's been by a few times today with a pretty serious look about her. You two getting serious, boy?"

"Lana's the one for me. Convincing her of it is impossible. She's got her mind made up that we're too different. I'm impulsive. How do I convince her I'm not?"

"You? Impulsive?" Emily burst out laughing, and Garrett looked at her. That wasn't funny.

She gave him a look that let him know she agreed with Lana's assessment of his character. He planned. Just because he had no problem improvising whenever necessary didn't make him impulsive. Necessarily.

"Honey, she's a pretty smart gal. I have a lot of respect for her, and her standards. She's a good girl." Emily took a deep breath, patted her neat hair. "I wonder if you know how you feel about her?"

"I want to marry her. Soon."

"That's my boy," said Jasper. "Since the old ticker's going to keep ticking, I'd like great grandchildren."

Emily interrupted, "Does she want to marry you?"

"I'm working on that." Garrett felt the engagement ring burning a hole in the front pocket of his jeans. "I'm asking her tonight."

"It's too soon, honey." Emily shook her head. "Can't you see she's skittish as a wild horse?"

"If I wait much longer, she'll avoid me and I'll lose my chance. She already bailed on the contract she signed. Went and did everything I hired her to do. I need her to think about me as much as I think of her. Besides," Garrett looked at them both, hoping they'd approve, "she may be skittish, but she likes me, and I like her. We have great chemistry, and I'm going to offer her to be my business partner."

Jasper looked at him, surprised. "Business partner? She's a pretty stubborn little filly, and I watched her work pretty hard these past years over there for Vivian. What makes you think she'd work for you?"

"Well, I'm still working on that…"

"Your Gran hoped you'd marry for love. She's full of silly romantic notions like that, but she was fancying you and Lana were falling in love."

"I love her." The words felt strange, and he knew he hadn't so much as hinted to Lana that he loved her. Hadn't wanted to scare her. She obviously didn't believe in love at first sight. If she did, he was in real trouble, cause it sure hadn't hit her the way it hit him. He'd be sure she heard the words tonight. He loved her.

"I know I want to spend the rest of my days with her, cherishing her sweetness, bringing out the warmth that hides just below her surface. I want to share the ups and downs a man and a wife face. I want family vacations, long cold winter nights, and the pleasure of seeing my woman wake up by my side. I don't want the kind of wife who will want to send my child to boarding school, who won't be there if he wakes up in the night with a bad dream. I want a family, an actual family, not one just in name. With Lana, with her sweet sensitivity."

Emily raised one eyebrow, then smiled at Jasper. "If you clean that up a bit, honey, that might be the proposal that could win Lana's heart. Just don't ask her in front of a crowd. Don't bully her. If you try to intimidate her into doing what you want, I fear you won't like the consequences."

"I won't. I have a plan." Garrett grinned.

Emily stood and kissed her grandson on the forehead, then clasped his hand. "I couldn't choose a nicer girl for you. As you know, your closer to me than my own son. I want you to have the kind of conventional life you always wanted. Try to let go of the frustration you feel about your parents and what they couldn't give you. I fear my son is not as warm and generous as you are, honey, but I'm proud of you. Lana's a wonderful girl. You have my blessing."

Garrett pulled Emily into a tight hug. "What you just said, it seemed to clear up a cloudy spot in my brain. You're right. I'm a grown man. I'm too old to be harboring resentments. I just realized I owe my parents a thank you for letting me make my own way. When I do something, it's genuine, because they showed me how I didn't want to be. I love you Gran, and I'm going to keep making you proud."

"You do. Jasper, don't get too excited. I'll be back to collect you for a nap in about an hour." Emily smiled at her men, then slipped out the door.

"So, I'm down and you swoop in and take over my business and my parties, eh?" Jasper looked at Garrett interestedly. "Planning a coup, then?"

Garrett told Jasper about the entire plan. Surprisingly, his Pap seemed even stronger than he had before his scare. He had a healthy flush Garrett associated with being alive, having another chance to accomplish great things.

He explained how Lana had set up the event and found himself more than mildly excited about the thought of dancing with her again. The next time he could get her in his arms would not be too soon. Everything should go well, since she arranged it. She could do anything.

When Garrett finished, Jasper sat back and said, "I can say I'm truly relieved you took over my business. I thought you might fancy yourself a big city chef. You always were a boy full of big dreams. Well, you're capable of anything you set your mind to, and your Gran has declared the rest of my time is hers now. If you convince Lana to marry you, everything should work out all right for you kids."

"You're a real pal, Pap," said Garrett, chuckling. He stood up, clapping his grandfather on the shoulder. As he was leaving, he heard him mutter, "Now get busy making me some great-grand children."

Lana slipped into the orchid gown, feeling strangely heady. She needed little makeup because her skin was flushed and bright. She realized she looked like a woman in love, and planned to tone that down. She was merely playing hostess.

Who wanted to be mistress of the host... not good.

Tomorrow she would loosen the ties Garrett was placing on her heart. Not that she hated the emotions he riled in her, it was energizing to feel so much. She wasn't certain yet how to handle the emptiness in the room—every room—without Garrett's enthusiasm to fill it.

To get it over with, she would have to get started, though. Tomorrow, tomorrow she would start. Tonight would be magic. The main floor of the Mill looked fabulous. This was her party too, and she was going to glory in it. Garrett's generosity and vision was making one of her wishes a reality.

Riverbend Falls old grist mill would have its place in history.

Chapter 16

She avoided Garrett most of the day. Yesterday she had dusted, cleaned, and decorated the old mill, and this morning she had drafted Tad and Kat to set up the folding tables she'd borrowed from the community center. She'd covered them with a fun variety of cloth and flannel backed tablecloths she'd saved up from various events.

Afterward, she'd gone to her own place to get ready. She was glad she'd taken her things from Garrett's earlier, so she was officially moved into her new old home. It was still in need of cleaning, but she planned to start that tomorrow.

For now, all she needed was just a place to crash. She was supposed to meet Garrett at the Mill at six to make any last-minute adjustments, but he'd showed up on her doorstep a half hour early. She'd been getting nervous now that everything was done, so she was grateful for the company.

Had she done enough work on the pamphlet she'd prepped for the town council? It would be imperative that Garrett get their support or the crew of old timers would make his life rough. They were good ole boys who didn't mind so much if the rules got broke, "just so's it's done respectful of the town." They didn't play by the rules either, if they didn't get their way.

Lana felt certain the extra emphasis she'd put on the fishing packages for seniors would ease their worries about Garrett bringing the evils of alcohol with his loose, easy ways.

Lana knew good and well they all fished with beer in their coolers. They were just posturing to see what he was made of. She knew he'd show them. It was all good. For Garrett.

She got what she wanted, too. Kudos for this account would boost her notoriety considerably. She could even freelance now, if she wanted, start her own business from the house.

Was she actually trying to pretend to herself that in any way she was going to be okay with not having Garrett? She kissed him. "Just trying to get into the act, boyfriend." Lana shut the big oak door and stepped outside, taking his arm. "Everything looks wonderful, doesn't it?"

"You seriously outdid yourself, babe. I still can't believe you pulled it all together so fast." They walked companionably across the large flat expanse between her front porch and the porch of what would be The Mill Bar & Grill. Guests would arrive soon.

"I just used what we had. All of this is possible because our neighbors and friends pooled resources with us, and that's just what we want to show them. That this is still the same Wilcox campground, just bigger, better, more accessible. Same good old-fashioned home-style place. It's gonna be a hit!"

Welcoming fires glowed in the antique lanterns she'd brought from her house. She'd always known her dad collected old things, but when she'd been hunting that aerial photograph, the wealth of vintage pieces from the old cotton gin and blacksmith building she'd found in the basement had been mind blowing treasure. Lana had chosen several special antique pieces to be on display tonight.

She'd hung the twinkling white lights from last week's dance from the ceiling to create the illusion of starlight. She'd had a few picnic tables hauled inside for the food, with oil lanterns serving as centerpieces.

A roaring fire in the stone hearth provided the perfect touch to the ambient light in the room. Near the hearth, Lana had spread out large green indoor/outdoor rugs from the dollar store and created the illusion of grass, then spread homemade quilts around the edges for picnickers.

A S'more station waited by the fire, offering mounds of marshmallows, chocolate and graham crackers to anyone with a sweet tooth who wanted to roast a marshmallow on a stick.

She had a smoker pulled up outside, smoking chicken and ribs. Kat made gallons of potato salad and macaroni salad, corn on the cob, and rolls. Lana would owe her big, later.

Emily snuck in a surprise tray of chocolate brownies. The cake was the masterpiece. Lana had the chocolate and vanilla sheet cake imprinted with the aerial view of the new resort layout. It was amazing what you could do with a photo reproduction these days.

Her scene was perfectly set.

As Garrett moved about the room, obviously pleased, she flushed with happiness. Instead of a suit, he was wearing khakis and a nice button-down shirt he hadn't gotten at Hank's. She grinned. He'd just wanted to go shopping with her. It wasn't fair, Lana thought, for a man to look that good.

"You look radiant, my lovely Lana. I'm glad you did this. I admit I was mad at first, since I wanted you to teach me what you do, but I can see why you balked at my terms. You think of everything, don't miss a trick, and all in with the whip of your little mermaid tail. I'm a lucky man to have met you, Lana Stone."

She felt a brief flash of apprehension when he said her name like that. Stone women were bad luck. Tomorrow. In the meantime, she'd have to try harder to tone down the radiant thing. "And I you, Garrett." She planted a firm kiss on his cheek and skipped off across the room as the first headlights cast their light through the window. "Good luck tonight," she called.

Good luck, Garrett thought as he touched the ring in the left pocket of his slacks for the millionth time. He watched her shimmy across the room and couldn't help swelling with the memory of how she'd rubbed that sweet body all over him half the night, driving them both nearly out of their heads.

Man, he wanted her. As his woman. He looked at what she'd done for him and knew it was meant to be. She definitely loved him back. This was love.

He turned to greet his first carload of guests and his smile faltered. Unfortunately, his parents hadn't heeded his request to leave him alone and take the hellcat with them.

His parents did not approve of public scenes, as he learned from several efforts during his childhood to get their attention. Inevitably, they listened blankly, chastised him about bad manners, then ignored him. He'd learned to indulge them. If they embarrassed Lana, though, he was going to let them have it, whether or not it hurt his reputation. Hopefully, a scene could be avoided.

The party was going wonderfully when Lana slipped out to be alone with her thoughts. Nearly ninety people had come. The presentation had been a success with the overwhelming consensus that everyone would be back with money in hand, relatives in tow. The food had been a hit, and Kat had a good crowd singing and dancing to karaoke on the "lawn."

She was standing just off the porch, staring at the river in the dark, listening to the cool trickle as it ran downstream. The warmer weather had held, and guests mingled about, telling stories about their kinfolk who had come to the mill for many years to process their harvests.

A lot of nostalgia flowed about the place, and several times people had mentioned how they missed her parents at this party every year. It was harder than she'd imagined it would be to come and be social after spending the night by herself for so many years.

"I can't understand what Garrett could see in her," said Cynthia in her annoying voice that Lana recognized easily. "She certainly doesn't compare with you, Felice."

When she heard Cynthia's sticky sweet voice, she'd started to move further away, but the conversation stilled her. It figured the two women would gravitate toward each other. Another reason not to like Felice. She was not an eavesdropper by nature, but Lana couldn't bring herself to walk any further away. She was the hostess here.

"He's playing with her. I am no worried. He'll return to me, and we will be married. No country bumpkin will have the husband I have chosen for myself. I believe he still loves me as much as he did when he asked me to marry him two years ago. I will make him beautiful babies. He wants heirs. I will be a lovely mother, so like my own Mother."

"They're always together." Cynthia said. "What will you do to remind him?"

"Wait and see. Garrett Wilcox is hooked on my charms, and even if that little girl teased him into looking at her, she won't long fill his voracious appetite. He's spoiled on French loving." She laughed then, and Lana felt wretched. "I do not see that they are together right now..." Felice's voice faded as the two gals disappeared through the heavy door into the mill.

The woman laughed beautifully. Lana ducked back into the darkness. Hanging back a few minutes, she did a few toe flexes in her pretty new shoes before straightening her shoulders and marshaling her strength.

So Garrett had lovers. Of course he did. He was a handsome, rich, clever, sexy—very sexy man. It's not as if those kinds of guys hang around waiting for nice girls to reject them. She had been right to guard her heart.

Climbing the steps heavily, she dreaded whatever Felice was planning. She nearly collided with a very antsy Emily, standing with Garrett's parents.

She had yet to meet his dad, and honestly, even after shaking the man's hand—Garrett's mother introduced her as Garrett's "friend"—Lana felt like she still had yet to meet the man. Wherever he was in his head, it wasn't here. Not even mild interest flickered in his eyes. Emily was watching Lana with concern as Garrett's mother neatly separated Lana for "a brief chat."

Madame Wilcox took Lana's hand and examined it, making Lana very nervous. "Well, child, I don't believe you're good enough for my son. Surely you realize you're cut from a different cloth? He from silk, you from burlap."

She patted Lana's hand as if she hadn't just walloped Lana with the insult of all insults. Lana was stunned. "Now see, there's a silk butterfly for my son. A woman who will know how to behave. They were to be married. His first love. He got cold feet and ran, left her holding his empty promise. My son will want to fulfill his promise to her. You won't stand in the way of their love, will you, Lana darling?"

Lana tugged her hand away, feeling as if she'd been holding a snake. She felt very cold. She would've needed to make a good impression on this woman who obviously knew how lacking she was. The sick feeling blew into full-blown nausea when she followed the awful Mrs. Wilcox's nod to the other side of the room, by the fireplace, where two women flanked her son—Cynthia against one arm, Felice cuddled against the other—whispering in his ear. He didn't seem to mind.

She looked back at Garrett's mother, then at Garrett, and squared her shoulders. He seemed to tell them a good joke. Probably the joke about how the country girl was no competition for French femininity, Lana thought bitterly.

Why should she care? Garrett wasn't really her boyfriend. He was just a lousy actor. Probably was a lousy real boyfriend. Lana wished she believed that. He was caring, and she wanted to be the girl he cared for.

"I'm so pleased to meet you, and I apologize for not being good enough for you. I can see you're a fine woman, simply by knowing your son. He's a fine man. Now if you'll excuse me, I really must go." Lana moved herself away from the mean woman, heading over to where Kat had the attention of most of the room now as she and Hank sang a pretty decent rendition of Elvis's "Hound Dog." Fitting.

As she walked away, she heard Garrett's father say to his mother, "She's not exactly what I expected."

No. Apparently, she didn't measure up for either of them. Oh, why did she have to fall in love with a man who had so many of his own complications? There was no place in his life for her. She understood, but she didn't like it.

Changing her mind about joining the karaoke crew, she pretended to see someone she knew by the door and changed directions, not looking in Garrett's direction at all. Why was she even here? Hoping for a night of magic? Was she crazy?

Lana tried to calm down, stopping at the fence that overlooked the river outside the mill. She didn't want to sleep all alone in the house. Not tonight.

She didn't want to face it until tomorrow. She cried quietly, hot tears that snaked silently down her face and then hiccupping sobs she couldn't stop. Thankful for the ever-present tinkle of the flowing river, no one would hear her if they just stepped out. In a minute, she would go home. Had to get started. She just couldn't get a hold of her emotions. They didn't suppress anymore the way they did before. There was such intense discomfort in her chest, she thought she was having a heart attack. She cried harder.

She was nearing exhaustion and all cried out when she felt a gentle caress on her arm.. Garrett was beside her, sliding his jacket around her shoulders. His breath warmed her. She was surprised he had noticed her absence. He stood there a moment, just offering closeness and strength before he spoke.

"I've been trying to get away since I saw you dart outside after talking with my mother. She wouldn't tell me what she said to upset you. Just ignore her. She's a selfish woman, and I told her so. I think my father might have just told her so for the first time in her life as well. You should have seen it." He paused a moment, then laid his hand gently on the back of her head and pulled her closer until Lana relaxed into the cocoon of his embrace.

"I'll be fine, Garrett." Lana snuggled closer, her response muffled by his chest.

He squeezed her tighter. "I want you to be honest with me, Lana. You can talk to me."

Lana shushed him. "I don't want to. I don't want to talk about anything." She bit her lip tearfully, wanting to say everything and nothing. Their situation was hopeless, but she noticed he'd left the party and come for her, even with France's finest on the prowl. She must mean something to him, but Lana was not wife and mother material, was she? Could she be?

"I'm not going back. You'll need to get back to your guests," she said, hating the idea of being left alone again.

"We're off duty for the night. I stopped and talked with my grandparents on the way out, made our excuses for the evening. Will you still stay with me at my place tonight? And then tomorrow…"

She interrupted him by catching his bottom lip in her teeth, then kissing him, a sensual invitation. "I want tonight to be a beautiful memory I can take out and cherish for years. I don't want to talk about tomorrow."

"Oh, Lana, I want to cherish—"

"Garrett, please," she interrupted. "No strings. Let's have a magical night, please?" She looped her arm through Garrett's on the way to his rig and they drove back to his cabin in the bright moonlight.

She squashed the knowledge that everyone at the party would notice both host and hostess disappeared before ten, long before midnight, but she didn't care. She was going to spend this night with the man she'd lost her heart to and enjoy every minute.

When they arrived, he walked to the passenger door and scooped her up as if she were a child. She didn't want to be turned out of his arms. His embrace felt so warm and safe, and she felt so cold before he came.

He must have sensed her need for closeness, because he held her tight. He walked confidently and quickly down the little path to his cabin, mumbling sweet words. Lana knew she was as close to heaven as she could get in this life, and her New Year's Eve only got better.

Garrett carried Lana to the back porch of his cabin. Lana felt a small thrill at seeing the well-lit hot tub bubbling and splashing. Garrett set her down on the edge of the tub and walked over to ignite the small fire he'd laid in the fireplace. A bottle of champagne sat in an ice stand next to her and there were candles and rose petals everywhere. Two huge, thirsty towels sat on a small bistro table next to a bag from Renee's.

Lana briefly wondered who would have come back with him if not her, but since she was playing the starring role in this romantic scene, she stifled the jealous thought. Romance was not something Lana was familiar with, and it felt wonderful. She felt no trace of the hopelessness she felt earlier. Now she would simply enjoy this for what it was.

She affected a playful smile. "Not to be a party crasher, because this party is more interesting than the one we just left, but I didn't wear a swimsuit under my dress."

Garrett chuckled and picked up the bag from the table. "This has too much coverage for my taste, but I thought you might like it, and I might like you in it. I insisted on a two-piece." He laughed when she playfully splashed a little water from the hot tub toward him.

"And why do you suppose I need a two piece?" Lana asked, giggling.

"Surely you enjoy showing off your fabulously toned ab muscles. I wouldn't want you to feel cheated." Garrett began unbuttoning his shirt.

She watched, fascinated, still wrapped in Garrett's jacket, not wanting to take it or her clothes off, but wondering at the same time why she would resist. She wanted this, to lie next to him, to touch every inch of him all over again. The black hair that matted his chest was so sexy to her she wanted to lay her cheek against it, just one more time.

She stood watching him, apparently transfixed, and Garrett watched her, finding himself aroused to know she was holding her breath, waiting for him to take off his shirt.

"So would you care to ring in the New Year from the relative luxury of a hot tub?" Garrett asked, deciding to move slowly. He removed his shoes, hoping she'd agree. She was wound up tight. He really wanted her to want him. And she would, he felt certain. The emotion he felt just being in the same room with her was tangible, and he wanted to share it with her for all time.

"Are you warm enough now?" he asked, moving to throw another log on the fire.

Lana started out of her reverie. "Sure, I was just wondering how much smaller a suit would have to be to show the amount of skin you prefer. This is lovely, though. I'm surprised you thought of it." She shrugged out of the jacket, folding it neatly near where he'd begun dropping his clothes.

Garrett stood and kissed her briefly, catching them both by surprise. He pulled away just as abruptly, muttering that he was sorry. He was moving toward the champagne stand before the surprise even registered on her expression. Now he was the one acting crazy, hot and cold.

"Why don't you change, and I'll fix us some bubbly," he said as he picked up a fluted glass. He hoped she would say yes. If he hadn't blown it by kissing her. He hadn't meant to kiss her. Yet.

She was supposed to get comfortable. Then he'd ask her. The unfulfilled need for her hurt like a bad stomachache. The only thing better than having her in his bed tonight would be having her in his bed every night. Marriage was the perfect solution.

Chapter 17

"What a wonderful soak. Takes the tension right out of a girl," Lana said as she climbed unsteadily out of the hot tub just before midnight.

They had been talking about everything for nearly two hours as they soaked—the sky, the earth, their health, their past, their pain, their pleasure. Lana knew they'd bonded this night, and she hated the thought of starting her more mundane life without him tomorrow.

The thought was heartbreaking, but it helped to put off thinking about it. Not for the first time, Lana wished tomorrow would never arrive. I'll just be here, tonight, she thought, as Garrett stood next to her, both of their hands wrinkled from the water.

She would treasure tonight for the time they spent talking, learning to know each other. Garrett teased her, saying the sweetest things, probably hoping to get a rise out of her, but she kept her emotions in check—outwardly. He touched her hand, her cheek, her knee.

Her skin burned with longing where he touched her so casually. Lana was overwhelmed. She knew her resolve to remain aloof from his affection would crumble if she kept his company much longer.

She was confused by his casual behavior. Aside from kissing her, he had not made any passes at her, though the surrounding atmosphere had been sensual, even erotic. Stars overhead, hot water bubbling around them, the firelight flickering in the shadows of the room...

Garrett was aggressive, but since Felice had arrived on the scene, he seemed to tone that down. Still, he drove her body mad with frenzied longing for his passionate embraces. The kisses they'd shared in his office, on the doorstep of the cabins, on the streets of Riverbend Falls.

Those kisses meant something. They were deep, soul sharing experiences. If Garrett wanted to be casual now, that was okay, but she planned to get what she wanted out of this evening. She knew from the depth of his tender caresses that she wouldn't want to leave after sharing the intimacy of lovemaking, but she would.

She needed to be her own woman, not his Girl Friday. The irony was that she wasn't enough of a woman for him, and yet he wasn't enough for her. She would want to be his companion, his friend, his wife. His equal.

And there was the issue of children. He wanted heirs, and Lana was uncertain she was capable of motherhood. What if the jinx hurt them as a couple? Would they leave their children to the mercy of the world, the way she'd been left all alone? She came out all right, but she believed the best way to avoid the jinx was the solitary lifestyle she'd been happy with before Garrett danced his way into her life.

She shook her head, trying to clear the champagne buzz, and nearly fell over. Garrett draped a fresh towel over her shoulders, making a joke that he chuckled at. It was nearly midnight, Lana thought, nearly tomorrow.

She felt dizzy—champagne, heat, and hormones were doing a number on her. She knew in her heart that her life couldn't be complete without feeling alive the way Garrett made her feel. Maybe the light of a new day would offer them options. Tonight... well, tonight was for cherishing, no matter what happened tomorrow.

Garrett was enchanted… Lana's beautiful complexion was flushed and rosy and firelight danced off her blond highlights. Garrett knew their relationship could work. He knew it would. They could work together, at home and at work, or he would support her career any way she needed him to. At the stroke of midnight, he was ready to propose.

"Lana," he said, "I need to ask you something." The question was on the tip of his tongue when Lana stumbled over the towel he'd dropped on the floor. He barely caught her.

"No more talking," she said, her voice as smooth as the murmur of the river. She pressed her damp body against him and his coursed with desire. She kissed him hotly on the mouth, his jaw, nipping at his neck. Hot need flowed through their lips and the surrounding air sizzled. He cupped her firm bottom in his hands and lifted her closer, feeling a complete loss of control. The heat of the moment took over every thought. "Take me to bed," she said silkily.

"Are you sure?" Garrett was torn between his convictions and overwhelming passion.

"I'm sure," said Lana. "I just wish this moment could last forever."

"It can, my love," Garrett said as he secured her legs around his waist and carried her to his room. Her head lay against his shoulder. He laid her down and stood back, looking at her.

"Lana…"

"Quiet." Her voice was quiet, sleepy sounding.

"I'll be right back." Garrett took advantage of the physical space between them to clear the blind lust from his vision. He went to the kitchen to get some air and a glass of water. She needed to hydrate. Sober up a bit… she'd had a lot of champagne.

He would ask her to marry him now, before he made love to her. They would be engaged then and her self-respect would be intact in the morning.

He returned to find her curled up in the center of his bed, sleeping. She'd taken off her wet swimsuit. He knew because it was lying on his floor. She had nothing on but the sheet draped over her sexy silhouette. He desperately wanted to join her, but felt the blood rushing to his head. He'd have to sleep on the couch.

He set the glass of water on the bedside table and reached down to stroke her cheek, tucking a strand of hair behind her ear. She moved a bit, but her breathing remained slow and deep. Garrett sat next to her for a while, watching her move through the stages of a dream.

Before he stood, he spoke aloud to her as she slept. Confident and passionate, he asked, "Lana Mae Stone, marry me and be my wife, my love, my passion, my partner for all time?"

As he expected, she slept, breathing softly. Garrett went and lay on the couch he was spending so much time on, staring at the ceiling. Tomorrow she would agree to marry him, she would. Then they'd share a bed for all their days.

She woke up alone in his bed and Lana knew it to be a bad sign. She sat at his writing desk and penned two letters. No matter how much she cared for him, he would be too busy, always unpredictable, just too many variables with him for Lana to deal with.

He needed a secretary, not a complication. They would be friends. Maybe in the future he'd settle down enough that she could keep up, but she told herself being near his energy once in a while would be enough for her, for now.

She stepped out of his room after tidying up the bed and hanging the swimsuit to dry in the half-bath. Wearing her dress from the night before, she gathered her purse from the living room and stopped to stare at his sleeping shape spread out on the couch. He was snoring softly, but it didn't diminish the fact he was striking to look at.

It hurt her heart to know this would be the last time she would look at him like this. She needed to leave before day's light stained the sky with tomorrow. Now. If she waited to say goodbye, she was afraid she might not maintain her dignity.

Whatever affection he felt for her would fade with time, she knew, and then she would only be in the way of his voracious appetite. She wasn't a prude, but she was no love machine. He'd obviously found her lacking again, choosing to sleep on the couch rather than make love to her. She distinctly remembered asking him to, though she couldn't remember how she got to his bed. She'd had a little much to drink.

She couldn't bear the thought of not being good enough. She was good enough, if you counted her other strengths. Just maybe not what he needed. Her job was complete; she would get a good recommendation. All of her dreams would come true. Why did everything feel so rotten then?

She placed a whisper soft good-bye kiss on top of his head. She wanted to touch his tousled thick black hair one more time, but resisted, a tear escaping from her eye.

She would continue to love him despite fate's meant- to-be's. As she slipped out the door, the clear, cold night was a reminder that she still had time before tomorrow arrived, the tomorrow she would not postpone ever again. From now on all her days would be todays.

She left two letters.

The one she had for Jasper and Emily she placed on their door before walking up the road in the dark to her new home. She thanked them for being kind, taking her into their home, sharing with her the warmth and love of a family during the holidays. She'd appreciated them making her and Tad feel part of their family. She offered to help them move when the time came and advised Jasper not to work too hard on Emily's honey-do list, lest he not get much fishing done. She'd kept it light and sweet, like the couple themselves.

The letter she left for Garrett on his pillow had left her emotionally wrung. She'd been deliberately hollow and trite, made nice comments about working with him, and how he could call on her services in the future. Wishing him happiness and despising herself for it. She didn't wish him happiness without her. She didn't want to assist him with future projects. She wanted more time…

The man had issues, too, she could tell. She recognized them because she had so many of her own. Maybe, someday, they could grow to be right for each other, but not yet. For heaven's sake, his ex-fiancé was staying in his guesthouse. Clearly, he had his hands full, and running the resort was going to take an incredible amount of work, even for someone as hardworking and gregarious as Mr. Wonderful.

She could give him nothing more. This was a time for her to grow and stretch her wings. If only she would stop picturing Garrett in this growing she was supposed to be doing. He'd been a catalyst for her, enriching and encouraging her in her strengths, bossing her into things she didn't care to do.

He needed a clear head for decisions, and dealing with Lana's emotions would only make things more difficult. She just barely handled them herself. How could he handle how meticulous she was about everything? The man threw Armani on the floor and kept candy in dresser drawers. They both had a lot of growing up to do. She could give him nothing more.

He could not know she'd lost her heart to him. Her pride would not allow it. It would only make the impossible harder. She would not look back. She would not have to come this far down the road for any reason other than to see Garrett or rent a canoe from him. They could be neighbors while their lives went on. He'd probably marry Felice. Lana would get a dog, maybe pick up a man down by the river who looked every bit as impressive as Garrett did with his shirt off, or maybe she'd glimpse him working occasionally.

Impatient with herself, she walked on, knowing her heart would remain, but looking forward to feeling less ruffled. She'd been carrying foolish baggage far too long and only recently realized she needed to handle things as they came. One day at a time.

Her world had changed since meeting her impulsive employer. She'd learned to love and wryly wondered if it could be any more painful. When she unlocked her dark house, she despaired at the loneliness. If only she hadn't walked through the halls with Garrett, watched him touch his fingers to unique patterns in the wood grain, watched him draw a smiley face in the dust on an old mirror.

She'd forever be imagining him in the space, bringing to it all the richness with which he seemed to see the world. Lana was frustrated and depressed, and thought maybe she'd ask her brother to come out and stay with her for a day or two, for old times' sake.

She grabbed her duffel bag from against the wall so she could change and walked around the ground floor, turning on all the lights. She loved the large dining hall with the oak table her Dad built for her Mom, but their bedroom she passed by for now.

Her bedroom... it was the one she'd take again. Her bed was still against the wall. She needed new sheets and bedding for all the rooms, she told herself, starting a mental list. For now, she'd clean to settle her nerves.

Outside the kitchen, she stopped, leaning against the doorjamb, and looked around the room. Not modern, except maybe the oven, but definitely functional. Deep wide counters, an island with a couple of bar stools standing like ancient sentries in the center of the room. A pantry—empty now—but her Mom had always kept it full... baking supplies, canning jars, pickles, tomato juice, green beans they'd snapped and canned together.

She pulled a stool up to the island and sat down, studying the cleaning supplies she'd lined up. She put her head in her hands the way she'd often done when lamenting to her Mom about some tragic crush gone awry.

She spoke aloud to hear the comforting words of a time gone by. "And if you don't mind me saying so, you act like you've had your heart broken, Lana. Are you just going to flop around and die on the bank, or ya gonna flop back into the river? Keep flowing, baby. Ya gotta flow. Don't let no boy see he's broken your heart. Just forget about 'em. If they don't come a knockin', they weren't worth having, child."

She stood up then, eyes closed, picturing her parents, and smiled from a sweet spot where she kept her finest memories.

Lana's Leap

Finally, they rested peacefully in her mind.

She would make their home hers. Some part of her whispered about family. She wanted a family to share her home with. Unbidden in her mind came an image of Garrett, a little girl holding his hand as they stood near the river. A little girl to fulfill a prophecy and break the jinx. She wanted him to be with her. Why couldn't she just take him? Why did fear of failure dog her every decision?

"I'm going to keep flowing," she said to herself, opening her eyes, flexing her shoulders. She wasn't the kind of girl who gave up when something got hard, she got organized, and tackled it one problem at a time. Lana got out her mental box and put all her problems in it. She got out a duster, a broom, and a mop, and cleaned out her house and her box, one room and one problem at a time.

Later, after a lot of hard work, a few tears, and finally laughter, Lana felt better. She would be all right. She was grateful for a beautiful first day of the year to make her feel light and optimistic.

They predicted a cold front for the next day, but today, sunshine would glisten off the waves. She reminded herself over a glass of iced tea that she was a strong, talented, creative woman, and now she had learned to love. After her heart healed from missing Garrett, she would get on with her life, and it would be good.

With tight and tired muscles, she thought she might take a walk before she laid down for a little while. The long hours she'd been putting in were catching up to her. She was still filled with nervous energy, though. She tugged on her jacket and as she was about to open the door, there was a knock on it. Her brother and her dream guy stood on her steps. Garrett had... a puppy?

Her private agony evaporated into confusion as the two boys entered her foyer.

"Look who I found, sis. I'm headed to Springfield today, and I wanted to know if you wanted to go..." Tad grinned. "I can tell by the way you two are looking at each other, you've got other things on your mind, so I'm gonna head on. I'll stop in later, sis."

When neither Garrett nor Lana said anything that sounded like words, Tad left. Lana barely noticed as he quietly shut the door. They stood in silence, but Lana was so pleased he'd 'come a knocking.' The only sounds were the muffled grunts of the big-eared puppy in his arms.

Finally, she spoke. "You came? Why?" She moved toward him, his stormy eyes clouding. "That didn't come out right. What I meant was it feels like ages instead of hours since I saw your smile, and..." her voice trailed off. "I missed you already."

"Let's go for a walk." His features relaxed, but not much. "I've things to say to you, things I would have said properly if you hadn't run away in the night." His voice was full of hurt, accusation.

"Let's walk, then." They walked toward the river, the puppy trotting along beside them to the place where she used to play mermaid on the bank. "You know I'm an early riser. It was morning. Time to leave," Lana said defensively. "I was just following my schedule."

Garrett raised his chin and stared at her, a disbelieving expression masking his features.

"Well, perhaps I left quickly, but what difference does it make?" Lana said roughly. "Do you think it would have been better to see me cry? What were you hoping for? You became a part of my life in a short time, and I've not yet decided how I'm going to get along without you, but I will. I will..." she trailed off, her eyes filling up with tears.

"Why?" asked Garrett, moving closer to embrace her. "Why must you always do everything by yourself? I have ideas, plans, a way for us to be together. If you could just bring yourself to want to be with me, I'm in love with you, Lana."

She leaned into his strength, holding on because she had been so afraid she would never feel his arms around her again. It took a few moments for his words to filter through the emotion she was feeling, and she leaned back to study his face. He bore a hard expression, but there was a hint of hope too, and Lana didn't understand.

"Plans? What are you talking about? I can't very well... what are you talking about?" she asked, telling herself to shut up and listen for once. If he came for her, surely she could trust him to follow whatever plans he had made to buy them more time together. He had trusted her when it mattered.

"I wanted to ask you this at midnight, when I knew we were both truly speaking from our hearts, but circumstance didn't allow for it." Garrett was looking at her with the same hot accusation in his steely blue eyes.

Lana looked down guiltily, remembering shushing him when he wanted to talk to her. But a girl has to watch out for her heart and she had every right to protect herself.

Garrett took her hand and brushed her cheek with his other hand. She gazed into his eyes, feeling a little lost. Helplessly, happily lost. He took a step and went down on his knee in front of her. She felt her heart pound, pound, pounding in her chest. She never believed something this romantic could happen to her. Her dark knight had come for her.

Garrett pulled a ring from his pocket and held it clenched in his hand. The puppy sat looking at him with soulful eyes. "Lana, I've thought of a thousand ways to say this, to trick you, to tell you, to ask you. I still don't know how to describe what I feel other than to say since the first time I saw you across the dance floor, you changed my life. I'll not lie. I've wanted you since the first time your lips touched mine that night."

"Garrett, I know..."

"Lana, I need you to know I value your thoughts and feelings, and I've known for a while now that no small amount of you would do. I love you. Will you marry me, share the rest of your life with me? Be my wife."

Lana stared for a moment, filled with emotion, mostly fear and love.

"Yes," she said, speaking from her heart. "I love you, Garrett. I've been so cold inside since you last kissed me."

She laughed, letting loose the flood of emotion she always carefully maintained, and Garrett scooped her up in his arms and whirled her around, stirring the puppy into a happy barking spree. His lips were on hers and the passion she felt made her heart pound with a new awareness of him, intensified to new heights.

"It will change our lives. I have a lot of peculiarities." Lana looked at Garrett, afraid for the future again. "I'll have to give notice at the office, because you'll need a lot of help, and I hate to… never mind," she said firmly. "Being with you is what I want, at any cost." In a quieter voice, she added, "Thanks for coming for me. I didn't want to think of us not being together. It hurt, here, in my heart."

"Babe, your depth continues to surprise me. You'd be willing to give up your all-important career for me?" He looked deep into her eyes, surprised at the truth. He thought she would refuse him, both as wife and partner. This was better than he dreamed possible.

"Garrett, I love you as much as I have ever loved another. You helped me to learn who I am, and I like who I am. I long to be with you. I would give up all I have gained these last months if I didn't take you for my mate." A tear rolled down her cheek and Garrett caught it with his lips, gently smoothing it away.

"I have to ask you about Felice. If her type is your type…"

"You're my type," Garrett said. "I won't ask what you heard, but I admit I had history with her, but it's ancient history. She's delusional, what my Gran refers to as a "climber and clawer."

Lana smiled, "Actually, I got that impression, too. But I overheard her say you were looking for heirs. I'm not sure I'm mother material. There's still the jinx to contend with."

Garrett cut her off. "I know you, Lana, and if you want to be a mother, you'll be a good one. If you don't want to, that will save us a lot of money." He grinned when she smacked his arm. "Seriously, I want what you want."

"OK," said Lana. "Are there any other surprises I need to know about?"

"I don't expect it to surprise you that I also want to ask you to be my partner. We'll work together and share everything, fifty-fifty, in every way. How I feel about you, Lana, has nothing to do with business. I just see a way for us to fulfill our lives side by side."

"You want me to be your partner?" Lana asked slowly, considering. "I thought you had to have an assistant, someone who follows orders?"

"Don't get me wrong, I'll still be bossy. I'm just saying when you boss me, I'll see what I can do to be a little less difficult." Garrett pushed at his rogue shock of hair nervously.

"OK," Lana said, "but we have to work together, decide things together. And hmm... will you be mannerly?" she teased, giggling when he tickled her. Her heart lifted. She felt so invigorated by his love.

"We won't be able to take a honeymoon right off. The whirlwind you ignited last night will need tending for a bit. The phone was ringing off the hook this morning, people asking to make reservations."

"Let's get a justice of the peace to marry us next weekend right here at this spot, where I first laid eyes on you. We'll honeymoon on the top floor of our new home." Lana smiled mischievously, wrapping herself in Garrett's arms, her body folding into his the way it seemed to when he held her. "I think I'm conceding the no touching rule, partner. No way I'll be able to keep my hands off you now."

Lana's tone was playful while his hands wandered down her shoulders, nudging at the skin under her shirt, his thumbs tracing a hot line at the top of her jeans. His silent strength had her hips arching into him, seeking more.

"Fair enough. I knew I'd like being partners with you." His black hair fell over his eye when he flashed her his cocky grin, and she felt lucky.

"You're amazing," said Lana. "I never thought I could let go again and have fun. You've helped me to remember why life is good. I'm content, happy for the first time in years. Deep down, I know what I want. No more doubting. I owe you for that."

"No, my love. You made your own destiny. Thanks for scheduling me in."

Garrett kissed her then, and she knew for certain whatever the curse threw at them, if Garrett was wrong, and being a Wilcox didn't beat it, they would navigate it together. Her heart was swollen to bursting with love and her mind was intrigued with the promise of their exciting, albeit unpredictable future. Beyond them, the river flowed, steady the flow, promising new life and love in the hills of Riverbend Falls. As their lips parted, Lana thrilled to the hungry look in his bedroom blues.

"Husband-to-be…" She gave his arm a tempting tug, then nudged the puppy in the direction of the house, "right now, indulging in you is at the top of my work list. We've got dreams to fulfill and plans to make… together."

CHECK OUT JAIME'S STORY
Planting Jasmine
Riverbend Falls ~ Book 2

RELEASE DATE: SUMMER OF 2023

Jaime Summers dreads her next contract in the historic mill town of Riverbend Falls, Missouri. When you fire people for a living, you don't tend to be popular, and this restaurant job is outside her usual element. When you fire people in the city, they find other jobs. It will require trickier maneuvering in her old town, where she already has a bad reputation. While she expects these 100 days of summer to be unbearable because of the humidity—she never considers a hot rancher might scorch her heart with the heat of love.

Tad Stone's passionate disapproval for his sister's best friend surprises him as much as the hunger that builds when she first locks her coy aquamarine eyes on his. She was to be part of the madness that has overtaken his town not that resort fever has transformed the serene river he'd grown up fishing and canoeing. It was turning into a tourist mecca complete with drunken boaters, the resulting flesh fair, and the litter left behind. As a divorced novice rancher with two young sons, he considered Jaime Summers trouble, but darned if he could help the desire to shake up his life—and have a little taste of trouble.

Delilah's Diction
delilahsdiction@gmail.com
www.delilahsdiction.com

Delilah Dewey writes genuine small-town romance during the small hours of the morning before heading to her satisfying day job in banking. In addition to collecting characters for stories, she loves to do research!

When she isn't working at a computer, or enjoying the day with her own romantic hero, she can be found cuddled up to a book, daydreaming about warm summer days, or putting on boots and gloves and tackling whatever project comes up.

Her favorite pastimes include outdoor fun, especially tent camping on the river, critters, and campfires.

Books written by Delilah Dewey
Published by Delilah's Diction

Lana's Leap

Visit the Author Page on Facebook

or visit my website at

delilahsdiction.com

Made in the USA
Columbia, SC
10 November 2023